Jo Macauley

Secrets
& Spies

Treason

With special thanks to Martyn Beardsley

First published in 2013 by Curious Fox,
an imprint of Capstone Global Library Limited,
7 Pilgrim Street, London, EC4V 6LB
Registered company number: 6695582

www.curious-fox.com

Text © Hothouse Fiction Ltd 2013

Series created by Hothouse Fiction
www.hothousefiction.com

The author's moral rights are hereby asserted.

Cover design by samcombes.co.uk

ISBN 978 1 78202 040 0

1 3 5 7 9 10 8 6 4 2

A CIP catalogue for this book is available from the British Library.

Typeset in Adobe Garamond Pro by Hothouse Fiction Ltd

Printed and bound by CPI Group (UK) Ltd, Croydon, CRO 4YY

With special thanks to Jane

Prologue

London, 4 November 1664

In the eerie half-light before dawn, the ship drifted through the autumn mist like a restless ghost. John and Will caught their first glimpse of it as they rowed their little boat through the vapoury grey swirls. The brooding turrets of the Tower of London rose out of the haze on their left. John shivered as he thought of the last time he'd been there two years ago to watch the execution of Sir Henry Vale, one of the men who had signed the death warrant of Charles I. He shook his head to rid himself of the gruesome image and turned his attention back to the vessel that lay straight ahead of them. Its

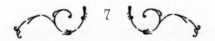

black hull and naked masts were silhouetted against an arc of brightening, star-speckled sky.

"What do we know about it?" John asked in a hushed tone, as if afraid he might wake the slumbering monster.

"Naught," Will replied. "Some of the watermen thought it was one of our warships come loose from her moorings, but all our vessels are accounted for. Mister Jones asked me to take someone to investigate before it causes a collision." He glanced at John's hands. "Are you trembling?"

John frowned. "'Tis just the cold – and the early hour. I should still be in bed."

"Let us get this over with quickly then," Will said. "I'll get on board and throw you a line, then we'll tow her to the bank and find a mooring post somewhere."

With frozen hands, they pulled harder on their oars until they had drawn alongside. The black wooden hull of the mystery vessel towered over them. There were no signs of life on board, just the mournful creak of timbers and the occasional slap of wet rigging against the mast. A spiral of mist curled its way into an open porthole like a probing finger.

"Will…?"

"What?"

"Do you … do you believe in ghost ships?"

"Oh, don't start…"

"But something doesn't feel right."

Will shook his head. "She's just a leaky old tub whose mooring rope has parted. Look."

Will reached over and banged his fist against the side. A raven they hadn't noticed, perched in the darkness at the end of the foresail yard, took sudden, noisy flight. Will jumped, almost overturning their boat.

"Naught to be scared of, eh?" smirked John.

Will ignored him and glanced up at the side of the ship. "Let's find her name."

They rowed along the side of the huge, dark shape. The ship's name was at the bow, picked out in blood-red letters against the black timbers:

DOODGAAN

"What does it mean?" John whispered. "It looks Dutch." He shuddered. A war with the Dutch was looming — everyone in the Navy knew it. Could an enemy ship have made its way to the very heart of London?

There was a sudden swell on the river. Their boat bobbed from side to side and the great black ship rolled so that its foremast swayed above their heads. Somewhere

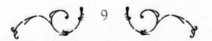

on deck something fell with an echoing bump and rolled across the planking.

"Let's just get her to the river bank," said Will, no longer sounding quite so chirpy. When their boat had stopped rocking, he stood up and reached into the stern for a coiled rope with a grappling hook at one end. Taking careful aim, he tossed the hook up and over the ship's side-rail. It landed on the deck with a clatter, which echoed across the river. They both paused for a moment, as if they expected the crew to come scurrying to the side to see who was boarding their ship. But the sound was quickly swallowed by the curtains of mist. Will pulled on the rope and, satisfied that the hook was fast, put one foot against the *Doodgaan*'s side.

"Careful," John urged, holding onto the end of the rope as tightly as he could.

Will shinned his way up, wrapped his arm round the rail at the top, and then hauled himself over onto the upper deck. John could just make out his grey outline as he peered back down.

"Nicely done, Will," he called. "Now find a line and let us shift ourselves from here."

"I'm going to take a quick look around…"

"What? No!" John cried. "Just find a mooring rope

 10

and let us leave!"

But Will had already vanished, leaving him shivering in the boat. He gazed at the slowly lightening sky and the stars flickering out on the eastern horizon like spent candles. He heard Will's faint footsteps on the deck as they gradually faded to nothing. Had he gone below? Why would he do a foolish thing like that? John waited and waited. How long could it take to explore? What had happened down there? What if Will had tripped and fallen down the hatchway into the hold?

An unearthly shriek from deep within the black hull rang out across the river. John's muscles froze.

"Will?"

There was no response.

He stood up and tugged on the rope so that the grappling hook would make a noise Will might hear. There was no response. John felt he had no choice – he had to go up there himself. A voice inside his head shouted that it was a foolish thing to do, but he ignored it and got to his feet. As soon as he prepared to climb, the rope went strangely slack in his hands. The grappling hook shot down towards him, striking him hard on the side of the head. John collapsed onto the floor of the rowing boat. Then everything went dark…

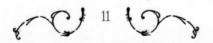

Chapter One

The Enemy Within

"Oh, really – this is *too much*!"

Benjamin Lovett tore off his wig and threw it down like a spoiled child, then stomped to the edge of the stage.

Centre-stage, Beth ran her fingers through her long, chestnut-brown hair, and gave a frustrated sigh. What was his problem this time? It was hard enough practising for a brand-new role without one of her fellow actors throwing tantrums all the time.

"Benjamin, my dear," pleaded William Huntingdon, the theatre manager. "I really had hoped to get on to

Act Three before this morning was out. With the theatre closed for the bonfire celebrations on the morrow, we're running out of rehearsal time!"

"She just doesn't *live* the part," Lovett whinged. "When *I* used to play the role of Henrietta—"

"Huh!" Beth uttered involuntarily, interrupting him. Her face flushed with anger and her emerald eyes bore into him. She pictured herself sticking Lovett on top of the King's bonfire at the Tower tomorrow instead of the effigy of Guy Fawkes...

"Benjamin, Benjamin—" began Huntingdon soothingly.

"*Sir*, just because the law hath been changed to allow females on the stage, it does not follow that you must use them. In the old days, people were more than happy with my art – *my* Desdemona was a triumph, you will recall. Do you really think you would get a performance like that from *her*? And as for my Juliet, the Earl of Buckingham himself said that it was one of the most moving he had seen!"

"Made *me* weep right enough," muttered old Matthew the prompter, grinning slyly at Beth from his little box sticking up at the front edge of the stage.

But Beth was too angry to smile back. She hated the

13

way Lovett always tried to make her look bad. Although she was receiving better and better reviews for each successive performance, she was afraid that one day Lovett would get his way and Huntingdon would hand him a female role just to keep him quiet. It had taken her two years to fulfil her dream of becoming an actress and she wasn't going to go back to selling oranges without a fight.

"Benjamin, you were one of the finest players of female roles the stage has ever seen," said Huntingdon. "But people want to see *actresses* now, and there is none more popular in all of London than our Beth. The Duke of York's theatre pulls in more people because of their actresses, and so must we. 'Tis bad enough that they seem to know what plays we plan to produce almost before I do…"

Beth felt the back of her neck begin to prickle with excitement. Not for very much longer they wouldn't. Not if she had anything to do with it. For some months now, the Duke's Theatre had been getting sell-out audiences and glowing reviews for plays the King's Theatre had been planning to stage. No matter how quickly they rehearsed, their rivals always seemed to be one step ahead of them. Clearly one of their own at the King's Theatre was informing the other theatre of their plans. The question was, who? Since Beth had begun investigating, she had managed to narrow it down to two suspects. Unfortunately, Lovett was not one of them.

"She can't even walk like a woman!" he hissed, gesturing at her dismissively with his gloved hand.

Beth was taller than Lovett and athletically built. She looked at his podgy legs, balding head and potbelly and once again anger shot through her body like a flare.

"But I *am* a woman!" she exploded. "How can I not know how to walk like one when I *am* one?"

"*She* is a mere girl of fourteen, Huntingdon," Lovett continued, once again completely ignoring Beth.

"Well, she's prettier than you, that's to be certain!" Matthew chipped in. There was laughter from the other actors, and Beth allowed herself a smile. At least they were supportive of her. They understood how annoying old Lovett could be. If he knew she not only wanted to play female roles, but planned to *run* the theatre one day…

"Madam," said Lovett, finally turning to face her. "There is walking – and there is *stage* walking…"

"And there is stage *waddling*," Beth retorted, looking pointedly at Lovett's huge backside.

Lovett's bottom lip began to tremble, and Beth shook her head in exasperation. She knew only too well what was to come. He might not be the leading lady any more, but as far as Beth was concerned he was certainly the drama queen of the King's Players.

"I cannot work in these conditions!" Lovett wailed. "Such insolence! Such disrespect!"

"My goodness, is that the time?" Huntingdon cried, bounding onto the stage. "Let us take a short break for some refreshments. Back on stage in ten minutes for the final scene."

With an exaggerated sigh Lovett flounced off, dabbing at his eyes with a violet silk handkerchief.

Beth hurried backstage to her dressing room. Lovett's temper might have ruined yet another rehearsal, but at least it gave her the opportunity to finally discover who had been passing secrets to the Duke of York's Theatre.

Once in her dressing room, she began rummaging through her trunk of costumes. If her plan worked, she would surely be given a more important mission next time.

Beth knew that the reason she'd been asked to become a spy was because she worked in the King's own theatre. Her experience as an actress meant that she was an

expert in disguise and role-playing, and she was proud to serve her King, both as an actress and a secret agent. But she was growing a little tired of being given jobs that revolved solely around the theatre. Hopefully, if she got this job right, she would be asked to do something a little more adventurous next time…

Smiling determinedly, she pulled out a couple of old scripts, removing the pieces of string threaded through the top left-hand corners that kept the pages together. She quickly replaced one with a bright red ribbon from the trunk, and the other with a bright blue one. There wasn't much time – Huntingdon would be calling them back soon. The question was, would her suspects take the bait? Stuffing the scripts into the pockets of her skirt, Beth scurried into the wings where she came upon Robert Wright, one of the minor actors. "Have you seen Mister Baldwin?" she asked breathlessly.

He blushed deeply and suddenly. "I'm not … I don't … Who?"

Robert was almost the same age as Beth, but he reacted this way whenever she tried to talk to him. Normally she was sympathetic because, despite his shyness, he was polite and friendly – but now there was no time to lose.

"Please, Robert, where is Mister Baldwin, the

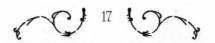

costume-maker?"

Robert's eyes lit up, glad to be able to help. "Oh … I think he just took Samuel's doublet to patch a small rip."

Beth doubled back towards Baldwin's room. The door was open, and she found him sitting on a stool, sewing. As usual he was wearing voluminous silk breeches and a felt hat adorned with gaudily-coloured feathers.

"Ah, Mister Baldwin," Beth called from the doorway.

"Why, it's sweet, darling Beth!" Baldwin declared, adopting the grandiose but insincere tone that always irritated her. He whipped a handkerchief from his pocket and wafted it around so that its lavender scent filled the air. Beth had never seen him actually blow his nose with it. "And what can Mister Baldwin do for his delightful young muse?"

Trying not to cringe at his ridiculous tone, Beth took one of the old scripts from her pocket. It was the one with the red ribbon. "Well, I've been learning my lines for our new production of *Love's Desire Spurn'd*, but I have to go back on stage in a moment, and I don't like to leave the script lying about … Could you look after it for me?" she asked, bowing her head slightly and smiling demurely.

"*Love's Desire Spurn'd*, eh?" Baldwin echoed, returning

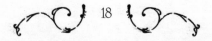

her smile and extending a heavily jewelled hand. He took the script from her quickly. "Certainly, Beth. It will be safe with me."

She felt sure there was a slyness behind his smile, but she had no time to waste dwelling on it. There was one more suspect to see...

After thanking Baldwin, Beth raced round to the front of the stage where Matthew, the prompter, was waiting in his box for the rehearsal to resume. She knew she had to act fast.

"Matthew, would you mind this script for me?" she asked. "It's for our next production, *Love's Desire Spurn'd*. Mister Huntingdon has been kind enough to give me a copy in advance, and I'm terrified I'll lose it."

As with Baldwin, Matthew seemed only too happy to oblige. "Anything for you, Mistress Beth," he said with a wink, taking the script that Beth had tied with the blue ribbon and stuffing it into the inner pocket of his jacket.

Beth hurried to her dressing room to fetch her sword for the final scene. The trap was set, and now she just had to wait and see what it would uncover. Red or blue ribbon? Matthew or Baldwin? As long as she kept her eye on both of them, she should be able to find out who had been selling secrets to their rivals. She heard

Huntingdon summoning the company back to the stage and gave a sigh. There certainly wasn't a moment's rest in this double life of hers. By the time she had scrambled back on stage, Huntingdon was already addressing the cast.

"This is the scene where Alexander and Henry are duelling over the beautiful Isabella. Alexander cuts off Henry's cloak revealing that 'he' is really the shapely Henrietta, who declares that she will never allow a villain like Alexander to marry her sister. Henrietta fights bravely but is defeated – dying speech, audience in tears, et cetera, et cetera. POSITIONS, PLEASE!"

Beth, who was playing Henry/Henrietta, prided herself on her ability with a sword. So when the fencing commenced, it was galling to see the smirk on Lovett's face as she had to follow the script and let him get the better of her.

"'Tis a love none can thwart, thou treacherous creature!" he cried with a ridiculously melodramatic sweep of his hand and tossing-back of his head.

The fight commenced, and after a few tentative lunges and parries Lovett made a strong attack and Beth pretended to stumble and fall, as the storyline of the play demanded. How she wished she could fight back, then

20

she'd show Lovett what she was capable of. She watched as he attempted a pirouette whilst waving his sword in a figure of eight. Halfway through the manoeuvre, he teetered and in one horrible moment she realized he was going to fall right on top of her. Quick as a flash, she rolled to one side and leaped to her feet. Lovett crashed down into a heap on the floor, and Beth noticed Huntingdon grimacing from the stalls.

But then something else caught her eye.

In the shadows at the very back of the theatre, two figures were hunched over in conversation. Something was being passed between them – something that looked very much like a script. But which one was it? Beth glanced down into Matthew's prompting box and frowned. There was no sign of him. But if she raised her suspicions now, whoever was responsible might hear her and vanish without being identified. She was determined to catch the scheming fiend guilty of the crime, refusing to let them slip through her grasp. Suddenly an idea came to her, and Beth's eyes narrowed. Now she knew exactly how to close the trap…

"You shall marry her over my dead body!" she called out to Lovett, resuming the scene.

"Ha! Then let it be so!" Lovett shrieked, heaving

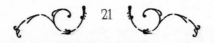

himself back onto his feet with a laboured grunt. He lunged towards Beth – but instead of letting him win she deflected his attack with her blade and quickly turned the tables on him, swishing and thrusting, causing him to stagger backwards. Lovett shot the theatre manager a panicked look, but ignoring his growing confusion, Beth continued her onslaught, her glinting blade flashing before his widening eyes. If only this could have been in the script – it was so much more enjoyable! Back and back she forced him, until they had fought their way down the stairs from the stage, and out among the seats where Huntingdon was sitting.

"Stop her!" Lovett screamed at him. "She hath gone mad!"

But Huntingdon was chuckling. "Inspired idea, Beth! Fighting all the way through the audience – they will love it! Defend thyself, Alexander," he cried, "for the honour of all men!"

Beth heard cheers from the actors left on stage as, in a blur of flashing blades, she pressed Lovett ever further up the aisle. The pair lurking at the back of the theatre were still too engrossed in their conversation to notice what was happening for now, but that wouldn't last much longer. She had to press home her advantage quickly.

Beth swished and lunged with ever more ferocity, until Lovett dropped his sword in panic and shuffled backwards as fast as he could, his eyes mesmerised by her flashing blade.

"Ow!" cried Lovett, as Beth prodded him in the chest. "Mercy! I beg of you!"

The two conspirators finally spun round, noticing the commotion, and Beth saw from the feathers on his hat that one of them was Baldwin. She didn't recognize the other man, who was holding the script with the red ribbon and looking horrified to see all eyes now upon him.

"Who is this man?" Beth cried, brandishing her sword at him.

"Why, 'tis Gilbert Sykes from the Duke of York's theatre," replied Huntingdon incredulously. "What's he doing here?"

"What indeed?" called Beth as Sykes hastily plonked the script into Baldwin's hands and ran for it.

Ignoring him, Beth bounded over two seats towards Baldwin, thrusting her sword through the script's ribbon and raising it aloft for all to see.

"A TRAITOR UNMASKED!" she yelled triumphantly as everyone gathered around. "Mister

23

Baldwin was passing the script of *Love's Desire Spurn'd* to a Duke of York's man!"

Baldwin tried to snatch it but Beth lifted it higher, out of his desperately grasping reach.

"*You*, Baldwin?" gasped Huntingdon.

"Why not?" Baldwin snarled. His usual insincere gaiety had vanished, replaced by a dark, murderous glower. "Milligrew at the Duke of York's pays me more for one little piece of information than you pay me for a whole month's sweat and slavery in that costume room."

"I didn't know we were doing *Love's Desire Spurn'd* next," queried Robert from the stage.

Huntingdon scratched his head. "Come to think of it, neither did I…"

Beth lowered the script and let it fall back into Baldwin's hands. "Did I say it was *Love's Desire Spurn'd*? Oh dear, my mistake. It appears to be my old copy of *All's Not Lost*, the play we performed last month!"

"You tricked me!" Spluttering with rage, Baldwin threw the script at Beth. "You'll pay for this, Beth Johnson, I'll make sure of it!" Then he turned on his heel and stormed off, the feathers on his hat quivering wildly.

"And don't come back!" shouted Huntingdon, to cheers from the cast.

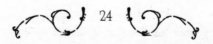

Out of the corner of her eye Beth noticed Lovett quickly pick his sword up and brush himself down when he thought no one was looking.

"We assuredly did a splendid job together there, Beth!" he declared. "The traitor exposed. His Majesty will be most pleased…"

There were a few giggles in the background, but Beth kept a straight face. "Quite so, Mister Lovett. You have worn me out with your swordplay. I now feel in need of some rest and refreshment, if Mister Huntingdon will allow it."

The theatre manager strode over and patted Beth on the back. "You have earned that and more, Beth. In fact, that's enough rehearsing for today. See you all later for the performance!"

"What have I missed?" Matthew called as he appeared from backstage dragging a prop horse behind him.

"Nothing much," Beth replied with a grin. She walked over to him and lowered her voice. "Could I have my script back please?"

Matthew reached into his pocket and produced the blue-ribboned script. "I was meaning to talk to you about that, Mistress Beth," he said. "See, the thing is, I don't think we're doing *Love's Desire Spurn'd* next. I'm

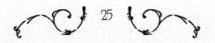

pretty sure it is—"

"Sorry, Matthew – my mistake," Beth interrupted with a smile, taking the script from his hand. "But thank you anyway." And with that she bounded off, leaving a puzzled-looking Matthew scratching his head.

As she made her way along the darkened passageway to the stage door, Beth's head buzzed with excitement. Surely after word got back about her doing so well on that task, she would finally be given a spy mission *outside* of the theatre? Something a little more daring and adventurous. Something in which she could use her sword-fighting skills would be good; she had really enjoyed her skirmish with Lovett. When she had first taken the job as a spy she had been even more nervous than when she made her stage debut, but with every success she had grown in confidence. Even Baldwin's threat hadn't frightened her. He was just a costume-maker, after all. What was he going to do, embroider her to death? She grinned to herself and sighed. Perhaps she would be given a job that actually brought her into contact with the King this time. That was why she had agreed to this double life after all – to help protect her King and country. Maybe she could be called to expose a Dutch spy, or…

As Beth opened the heavy stage door to leave the darkness of the theatre, a shaft of dazzling sunshine made her screw up her eyes, so bright that she was temporarily blinded … She didn't stand a chance against the figure charging down the alleyway towards her.

"NO!" she managed to scream, before the body slammed right into her.

Chapter Two

The Call of the Bells

"Let go!" Beth cried as she wrestled against her assailant on the dusty ground, trying desperately to free herself. Her attacker might not have been all that big, but what he lacked in size he certainly made up for in strength and determination, clinging to Beth like a leech.

Finally managing to wrench one arm free, Beth shielded her dazzled eyes and gasped in surprise. It wasn't a "he". It wasn't even an attacker.

"Maisie White! What on earth are you doing?"

"Oh, I'm so sorry, Mistress Beth, but I just had to hug you when I saw you were still alive!" the young

American girl gasped, gazing at her through a frame of shiny brown ringlets. In all of the confusion, her bonnet had been knocked sideways and was now perched on her head at an angle. Maisie released Beth from her embrace and helped her to her feet.

"Why would you be surprised to see me alive?" Beth asked, brushing the dust from her skirt. "I've only been rehearsing."

"I just met Robert Wright leaving the theatre and he said you'd been in a sword fight! With a man!" Maisie looked her up and down, as if expecting to see bloodstains on her clothes.

"It was only acting, Maisie! Well, mostly…" Beth grinned as she smoothed out her clothing. "And anyway, just because I was fighting a man, don't think it meant I was going to be the victim! I won hands down as a matter of fact." Beth began dancing around Maisie, brandishing a made-up sword, poking her friend lightly as though landing jabs. Maisie giggled, and in turn began to wield an imaginary blade of her own.

"I should have chopped his head off in one go!" Beth said with a dramatic swipe of her unseen blade. She charged up the alley swishing her imaginary sword this way and that. "I beat him back like a maid beating a rug, until he had no choice but to beg for my mercy!" She spun round and skipped back to Maisie, slinging an arm round the younger girl's thin shoulders, panting. They both laughed. "So you see, you didn't have anything to worry about at all."

"Thank heavens!" Maisie said. "It was hard enough fending for myself in Virginia after my mother died, and I don't want to go through it all again. You're all I have here – leastways 'til I find my father."

Beth hugged her closer. Maisie was just ten years old, a sparrow-like thing with a cute button nose and wide, eager eyes. She had been born in America after her English mother had been sent there on a convict ship. When her mum died last year, Maisie had stowed away on a ship bound for London, and Beth had found her begging in Covent Garden market. She took the girl under her wing, sharing her lodgings and finding Maisie a job selling oranges at the theatre, just as she had done as a young girl.

It was more than just sympathy that had made her do this – Maisie's story contained echoes of her own life. Beth had been forced to fend for herself at a young age too. Brought up by an elderly lawyer and his wife, who had found her abandoned on the steps of Bow

Church, the couple had given her a surname and a warm, safe place to call home. Things had been good, until each of them had died in close succession when Beth was still a young girl. She'd been left once again on her own, slipping through the cracks, and soon found herself exploited and made to work as an unpaid skivvy by disreputable sorts in the local area. Beth gritted her teeth at the memory, not wanting to dwell on it now. But running away to join the theatre had been her only means of escape from those dreadful times.

And then had come the chance to lead a double life of intrigue and espionage – or so she hoped.

Maisie had at least known her mother, though she too was now as good as orphaned. The girl clung to the hope that her father was still alive, though she did not know where he could be. She was desperate to find him, and had the names of some relatives who were supposed to live in London, south of the river. Beth had tried to help her to track at least one of them down, but with a common name like White it had so far proved fruitless.

"Don't worry, Maisie," she said now, squeezing her friend even tighter. "We'll get news of your father one day. We'll just keep looking. And nothing's going to happen to me, all right? Now, let's get home and take

some refreshment. I'm ravenous."

"Me as well. I've got us some ox tongues and venison pasties from the cook shop," Maisie said with a grin. "I think the man who runs the shop likes me. I play up to him a bit and he gives me some extra for free!"

But before she could reply, Beth heard a bell ringing out. She recognized it immediately as coming from nearby St Paul's Cathedral. The question was, how many times would it ring?

One, two, three…

"…I know how much you like venison…" Maisie continued, oblivious.

Four, five, six…

"…and the ox tongues were fresh in today…"

Beth held her breath.

Six times the bells rang … a pause, then one further solitary mournful chime.

Seven. Then the bells fell silent. Seven tolls with a pause after the sixth. That was her signal – one that had to be obeyed at all costs. Beth looked urgently up the street in the direction of the cathedral.

"What's wrong?" Maisie asked. "You do like a venison pasty – I know you do."

Beth saw the enthusiasm dimming in Maisie's eyes

and instantly felt guilty. "I'm really sorry, I've just remembered that I won't have time to eat. There's something I need to do first. Save some for me, all right? Here, I'll walk back with you, though. It's on my way."

Beth took Maisie's arm and they made their way down crowded Drury Lane. Like many of London's streets, it was too narrow for a pavement at some points and pedestrians had to compete for space with carts, carriages and travellers on horseback. But it was a short walk – the chamber they shared was on the first floor of the Peacock and Pie tavern, at the other end of the lane.

"Ah! Here's me babes!" cried Big Moll, the landlady of the tavern, as soon as she clapped eyes on them. Then she sniffed the air. "And what's that delicious smell you bring? Stopped by the cook shop, did you? Come, I have a table set up if you like…"

As her name suggested, Big Moll was a large woman. Very large. All brawny arms and wobbly white flesh – much of which, it seemed to Beth, appeared about to spill out like rolls of raw pastry from the low-cut dresses she wore. But despite her imposing appearance and gruff ways, she was caring and good-hearted: the closest thing to a real mother Beth had now. Even if, at first, lodging at the Peacock had just been a means to put a roof over her

head, Beth had soon come to regard it as a true home.

"Hello, Moll," said Beth. "Would you mind keeping my food warm for me? I'll be back anon. I just have something I need to attend to."

"'Course I will, me dear. I'll be preparing pies for the King's big Bonfire Night feast on the morrow. I'll keep yours right by the hearth."

Beth's skin tingled with excitement as she thought of Bonfire Night. It was nearly sixty years since Guy Fawkes had tried to blow up the Houses of Parliament in his infamous gunpowder plot. She always enjoyed the Fifth of November, when bonfires were lit all over London to celebrate the failure of his scheme, but this year she was looking forward to it more than ever. *This* year, she and the rest of the King's Theatre Company had been invited to the King's own celebrations at the Tower of London. Not only would there be the biggest bonfire in the whole city, but there would be a feast fit for a king – literally. Moll had been asked to provide pies as there were going to be so many people coming that the Tower kitchens needed all the help they could get. But secretly Beth believed the King had asked for Moll personally – it was a well-known fact that her pies were the best in the land. She wondered if he knew about Beth's own connection to both him and the renowned cook…

"Thanks, Moll. I won't be long, I promise," she said, her stomach growling in agreement.

"Good. 'Cos it don't do to go running about when you should be eating," Moll said with a wink. "Plays havoc with yer digestification."

Beth laughed. "I promise to keep my digestification calm 'til I get back."

"Can I come with you, Mistress Beth?" asked Maisie.

"Not this time," Beth said, avoiding Maisie's imploring gaze. She hated keeping things from her friend. After all she had been through, Beth guessed Maisie was probably canny enough to make an excellent spy herself, despite her age, but there was no choice. Not only was she sworn to absolute secrecy when it came to her spy work, there were just some things Maisie was better off not knowing about. She was a resourceful girl, but she could often get herself into trouble. "It's to do with a part I'm going to be playing," Beth continued. "I need to talk to someone about it."

In a way this was true. Being a spy *was* a role she played. It was just potentially far more serious and dangerous than her usual theatre roles. Beth wrapped her cloak about her and headed outside, pulling the deep hood as far forward as it would go. Her growing popularity on the stage meant that she was being recognized more and more these days. It was nice when people praised her performances, but there were times when she preferred to pass through the streets unnoticed. After all, it was this very ability to assume any role that had led to Sir Alan Strange, her mysterious spymaster, approaching her in the first place. When he'd appeared backstage one night – seemingly out of the shadows – and told her he had been watching her and had an unusual proposition, she'd almost told him where to go!

She smiled at the memory as she made the short walk from the Peacock and Pie to St Paul's: down Fleet Street, along Paternoster Row and up a narrow alley that opened out into the churchyard. She passed among the stalls of the booksellers and stationers, which had grown over the years into a little market around the cathedral, and quickly slipped inside.

It was quiet at present, which was good. One or two people at prayer were dotted about, and a group of fine-looking gentlemen strolled along the cathedral's lengthy aisle, deep in discussion. Either side of them were rows of immense stone columns; Beth's eyes couldn't help but follow them upwards. They seemed to soar into the sky, up to where the last rays of November sunshine poured in rainbow colours through the stained-glass windows. No matter how many times she came here, it was a sight that never failed to make her stare in wonder. Could there be another such building like it in the world? And now it was the place where she received her assignments from Strange. It had been only a year since her recruitment, and she still felt the need to prove herself.

Choosing her moment carefully so as not to be seen, she flitted among the shadows and quickly slipped through a doorway beneath the tall tower that dominated the centre of the cathedral. This door led into a little hallway that had three further doors leading off it. The one in the middle was locked and inaccessible to the general public – but not to Beth. She reached into her pocket, pulled out a large iron key and unlocked it, passing through and locking it again behind her. She felt her mouth go dry as she turned to look up at the wooden staircase that spiralled giddily above her head, then began the long haul upwards. Each time she came here she tried to count the number of steps, but always lost track long before reaching the top. Still, it helped calm her nerves. Even though she'd been doing this for a while now, each meeting with Strange still felt like those

first encounters had – intimidating and unpredictable.

By the time she had reached the platform, which ran round the bell tower like a narrow ledge at the top of a dizzyingly steep cliff, her legs and lungs felt as though they were on fire. A cold draught from the unglazed windows bit at her cheeks and passed right through her cloak, but from her lofty position she always enjoyed watching the sights below. She felt like an eagle patrolling the skies above the city, looking down through the plumes of chimney smoke upon the tiny people as they went about their lives, unaware of her gaze.

"Hello, Beth."

She almost fell backwards off the ledge in shock. A tall, foreboding figure stepped out from the shadow of the huge bells.

"Mister Strange! I came as soon as I heard the signal—"

"Did you succeed in your mission?" he said quickly. Spymaster Alan Strange wasn't one for small talk. He strode round the ledge towards her, his long black cloak billowing behind him in the breeze. As he drew closer, Beth couldn't help still feeling a little intimidated. The shadows in the bell tower always accentuated his strong forehead and deep-set, penetrating grey eyes. The pockmarks, lines and battle scars of his face reminded her of craggy rocks – the kind that ships got dashed against…

"Uh, yes, sir," Beth replied. "The culprit was Edward Baldwin, the costume-maker. He won't be back."

"Good. It was a simple enough task." Strange handed her a small bag of coins in payment.

Beth was about to inform him that it hadn't been *quite* so straightforward as all that, but caught herself just in time. It didn't do to contradict Alan Strange.

"Now, I have something else for you."

Beth's eyes lit up. Could this be the exciting task she'd been waiting for? "You have only to tell me," she replied without hesitation.

"Go to the offices of the Navy Board. It is within sight of the Tower, on Seething Lane."

"And they will give me further instructions?"

"Nay. They will not be expecting you," Strange said ominously.

Beth frowned. "I see … Well … actually, I don't think I *do* understand."

"You must make up a story in order to gain their confidence. Seek out a junior clerk, somebody who can be easily … *charmed*. I wish you to look into something for me without arousing any suspicion. It is to do with a

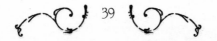

39

mystery ship that has appeared on the Thames, drifting, apparently deserted."

"Oh, just an empty ship...?" Beth's heart sank.

"I said *apparently*, Beth. I have reason to believe that there is more to this than meets the eye. Stay alert, and be careful. That is all for now."

Strange melted into the shadows without so much as a "farewell", leaving Beth gazing down from her lofty perch towards the broad River Thames. She wanted to believe that this new job would be of greater importance, but it seemed rather vague. Did Mr Strange yet trust her for the kind of *serious* spy work she had hoped to perform in the service of the King? If her previous jobs were anything to go by, she would probably find he had sent her to investigate the theft of a few ships' nails or rope. Beth sighed. She knew she had to be patient. Strange had personally chosen her to join his secret service, and would surely give her a big job in time – but it seemed unlikely some leaky old ship would be it.

Chapter Three
A Visitor

John Turner was beginning to wonder if he would *ever* make it to the quarters of his supervisor Arthur Jones. Because of the approaching war with Holland, the Navy Board offices were bustling with activity, and every step of his way brought some new kind of obstacle. Admirals, captains, officers from the victualling yard, clerks like himself – everyone seemed to conspire to get in his way as he battled through the corridors of the large, imposing building.

When he did finally make it to the top floor, John took a moment to straighten his clothes and try to get

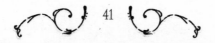

his breath back. Knocking on Mr Jones's great oak door made him nervous at the best of times, but now he had to tell his chief that he'd left one of his employees on board the mysterious ship they'd been sent to investigate. Will's scream still echoed in his head, taking John back to the river and the *Doodgaan*, its dark hull seeming to float not in the water but on a low-lying cushion of river mist. When he had regained consciousness, the mystery ship had disappeared – and Will with it. If it hadn't been for the huge bruise on the side of his head where the grappling hook had hit him, it felt as if he could have dreamed the whole thing. But he *didn't* dream it, and he urgently had to do something to put things right.

Taking a deep breath, he raised his hand and knocked on Mr Jones's door – but it was such a feeble sound there was no response from inside. It was always the same at times like this. Even after a year as a clerk at the Navy Board, John still felt like the poor boy from Shadwell who had been expected to follow in the footsteps of an ironsmith father who could barely read, or a grandfather who was an illiterate labourer. He tried again, this time overdoing it and surprising even himself by its loudness, which sent his heart racing once again.

"Who would knock my door down?" roared a voice

from inside the room.

John turned the knob with a trembling hand and crept in. Arthur Jones sat at a vast, highly polished desk and was surrounded by books, ledgers and sheaves of paper. He was a very thin man and he had taken to covering his pale, bald head with one of those huge wigs that had become so fashionable since King Charles had returned from France wearing one. Mr Jones's wig was a mass of auburn curls, which looked quite ridiculous perched on top of his little head.

As John shuffled into the room, Jones peered down his long thin nose at him.

"Ah, Turner. What of that ship?"

John could barely swallow, his mouth was so dry. "Well, you see…"

Mr Jones dipped his quill pen into an inkpot and continued with his work. "What, Turner? What do I see?"

John took a deep breath. "Something is very wrong, sir. With the ship."

Mr Jones looked up and raised one eyebrow. "Is she sinking?"

"No, sir. But I think there is something very bad on board."

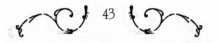

Mr Jones put down his quill and gave John his full attention. "What do you mean, 'very bad'?"

"I'm … I'm not sure, sir."

"You're not sure." Mr Jones shook his head resignedly. "Where is Will Brown?"

"That's just the thing. I think he's still on the ship, sir."

"What?"

"On the ship, sir. I think he's still there."

Mr Jones stared at him in disbelief. "Why on earth would you leave him there?"

"Well, I got hit on the head, sir. By the grappling hook," John leaned forward and showed him the bruise on his head, "when I was trying to go on board to get him. After I heard him scream."

Mr Jones's thin eyebrows knitted together. "Scream? Lord! I send the pair of you to undertake a simple task—"

"But sir! I mean, I'm sorry to interrupt, sir, but … well…"

"Oh, do spit it out, boy. I'm not going to bite your head off."

John wasn't so sure about that, but he had been given permission to explain himself so he had to use it wisely.

"Sir, Will is a very brave member of His Majesty's

Navy Board, not easily frightened…"

"Hmm, unlike…" Mr Jones seemed to think better of what he was about to say and stopped himself. "All right, I understand what you are saying. Pray continue."

John tried to hide his resentment. *Unlike you*, is what Jones had been about to say. But his supervisor didn't really know him. John knew he might look like a lowly clerk, but beneath his linen shirt beat the heart of a swashbuckling hero. Given the opportunity, at least. When he had joined the Navy Board, he'd had a vague notion that it would one day lead to him becoming a famous sea captain. But by the time John had realized that there was no route from the offices to the deck of a ship, his parents and six siblings had already come to rely on his pay.

"Sir, you must believe me when I say that I think Will must have seen something on that ship – something very frightening, very dangerous – to make him scream the way he did."

"I dare say it was infested with rats or something."

John shook his head gravely. "With respect, sir, rats would not frighten Will. Please, we must act quickly!"

Arthur Jones's expression softened a little. He rose from his desk and went to the window, gazing out as if he might see through the buildings down to the river. "Perhaps I should take this information to the Commissioner of the Navy Board," he said. "I have little doubt that Sir Roger Fortescue could make all the necessary arrangements to get Brown safely off the ship…"

John took a deep breath. "There's another problem, though, sir."

"What?"

"The ship."

"Yes?"

"It's disappeared."

Mr Jones looked at him sharply. "What do you mean, 'disappeared'?"

"Exactly that, sir. When the grappling hook hit me I must have passed out, and when I came to, the ship had gone!" John felt his face starting to burn.

Mr Jones started shaking his head really slowly, as if John was the most idiotic person he'd ever had the misfortune to stare across a desk at. "I am sure that Sir Roger will be able to locate it, Turner. It can hardly have gone very far now, can it?"

"N-no, s'pose not, sir."

"No, indeed." Mr Jones shook his head despairingly.

"Now, away with you to your book-keeping. There is a war coming!"

John ran back down the stairs to the clerks' office with a lighter heart. Although many sailors were away at sea, ready to fight the Dutch, plenty of them were still stationed around the Navy Board offices, and they could be deployed to take care of any difficulty Will might have got himself into. He made his way back through the bustling corridors with his head held high. There had been a problem but he, John, had solved it, even if he wasn't an officer who would actually board the ship to retrieve Will. Everything was going to be all right, he told himself as he returned to his office. Still, it would be strange to see the chair next to his empty until they…

John froze in the doorway and stared open-mouthed at Will's chair.

It was not empty.

He blinked hard but his eyes were not deceiving him. There was someone sitting as large as life in Will's place. Someone with a perfect, upright posture. Someone close to his own age, who radiated beauty and elegance. Someone who was wearing a dress!

Chapter Four

An Invitation

"You have a visitor," whispered one of John's older colleagues with a grin, as he strode past clutching a stack of files. "Much too pretty to be interested in you, though. Mention my name to her before she leaves, would you!"

In a room full of crusty, ink-stained clerks, even with her back to him the girl shone out like a beacon. The fading autumn sunshine poured in through the window making her red, silken cloak glow and her long, wavy, brunette hair shine like silk. Then she turned. Her glittering green eyes lit up when she saw John and she slipped gracefully from the chair and approached him with her hand outstretched.

Oh, Lord. Shake it or kiss it? Kiss or shake – quickly!

John reached out and was in the act of a clumsy handshake when the visitor helped him out of his dilemma by raising her soft, warm hand up towards his mouth. He gave the back of her hand a dry-lipped peck, then forced an awkward smile.

"You must be John Turner," the girl said. She had a clear, melodic voice. "They said you might be able to help me. I am to be in a seafaring play at the King's Theatre and it would help *so* much to know something of how the Navy works. My name's Beth," she beamed.

Beth! It was her – the one they were all talking about. Beth Johnson, here. Now. And he was still holding her hand!

Remembering his manners John quickly let go, causing her to laugh lightly, though not unkindly.

Some sort of words came out of his mouth, of that there could be no doubt. He just wasn't quite sure what they were, nor what they meant. If anything. But they must have been at least partly intelligible, because now she was thanking him.

"It's very kind of you, John."

He bowed deeply. "The pleasure is all yours –

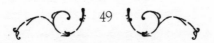

I mean, *mine*! Although, I hope it is yours too. But I don't mean that in a … that is, I do hope it didn't sound too…" He wanted to stop speaking, but his mouth just seemed to keep going independently of his brain, like a runaway horse.

Beth rescued him again. "There's no need to apologize and I quite understand what you mean. So, John, it must be such exciting work here at the Navy Board."

He shifted nervously from one foot to the other. "Oh, no…" he began, but quickly caught himself. He couldn't let Beth Johnson think he was just a boring clerk. "Well, not so much exciting as *hugely interesting*. And of the utmost importance to the nation!"

Beth's green eyes widened as she gazed up at him. "Oh, I'm sure it is! Will you be fighting the Dutch yourself?"

"Yes! Er, in a way. From a distance. The Navy must run smoothly, and someone must make sure of the, er, smoothness."

"Quite! And there must be interesting events happening all the time, rumours of invasions…"

"Daily!"

"Espionage…"

John glanced over his shoulder as if a spy might be creeping up on them right now. "Undoubtedly!"

"Sightings of strange ships…"

"Yes! In fact, only this morning I saw…" He quickly clamped his out-of-control mouth shut. What had happened that morning was something he didn't want to think about – let alone talk about. "Well, I *thought* I saw a mystery ship. On the river. But I was probably mistaken."

"Oh?" Beth held his gaze for a moment.

It felt almost as if she could read his mind, which was more than a little alarming considering what he was thinking as he gazed at her. He leaned on the edge of the desk to steady himself.

"But," Beth probed gently, "how can you be sure?"

"How can I be sure of what?"

"How can you be sure you were mistaken?"

John felt his cheeks begin to burn again. "It was – it was very foggy," he spluttered. "It could have been anything."

Beth nodded. "Floating along the river."

"Uh … yes."

"And what about the crew?"

"Oh no, there was no crew. Not a soul. I mean…" John squirmed. He felt as if he were a piece of mooring rope being tied in knots. An image of Will disappearing

51

below the deck of the mysterious ship popped into his mind. He clenched his hands together to try to stop them from trembling. "It's hard to say for certain."

Beth regarded him quizzically for a moment, then she smiled. "Well, you are at work so I don't want to trouble you further now. But perhaps we could meet later to discuss the Navy in some more detail?" She produced a playbill from her pocket with a brief note written on it and handed it to him. "I am currently appearing in this play. Show this to the stage manager after the performance and you shall be allowed to see me backstage."

Before he could even answer, she pecked him on the cheek, then turned and swept from the room with the grace of a cat, the poise of a queen, the radiance of an angel. In John's humble opinion.

As he took his seat, the predictable outburst of sniggering and teasing from his colleagues broke the normal industrious silence of the office. He didn't care. He barely even heard them. John Turner, most junior of junior clerks at the Navy Board, was going to the King's Theatre, Drury Lane, as the special guest of Beth Johnson!

Chapter Five

Behind the Door

Beth left the busy Navy Board building and emerged on Seething Lane with a small smile of satisfaction playing on her lips. Asking to speak to a junior clerk had proved more fortuitous than she could ever have imagined. She felt certain that John Turner had seen the mystery ship Alan Strange had asked her to investigate, but she couldn't really understand why he was acting so nervously. He was a tall, handsome boy – surprisingly so. His light brown hair and warm brown eyes were certainly appealing. But he was so easily flustered by her, it was almost off-putting. Although … perhaps she was overestimating her effect on him – perhaps there was something about the ship that he didn't want to disclose that had been making him so jumpy. She certainly sensed there was more than what he had told her. Still, what could be so scary about a ship that had run adrift?

Beth pulled her hood down over her eyes and began weaving her way through the noisy, smelly, teeming London streets. She made a special point of avoiding the central drainage channel that ran down the centre of many of them, acting like a sort of open sewer. She thought back to the way John's hands had started to tremble when she asked him about the ship's crew. What had he seen that had made him so scared, she wondered. Perhaps Alan Strange's hint that this might be a more important job was right after all.

Still, John really had struck her as the kind of boy who would be scared of his own shadow, so maybe it was all in his head. She frowned, pondering. If John came to the theatre tonight – as she felt sure he would – she would get to the bottom of it, and then, surely, her spymaster would trust her with a truly thrilling and intriguing task?

She crossed over to the other side of the street. A small church squatted in the shadows of a huge wrought-iron gate. Beth felt a chill run through her whole body as

she looked up at the stone skull and crossbones glaring down at her from the top of the gate. With fearsome spikes protruding from the top of each skull, it seemed more like a prison than a church. Beth thought of the warm and cheery Peacock and Pie with Maisie waiting, and she pulled her cloak tight and hurried on her way.

John peered down into the gaping black hole that was the Doodgaan's main hatchway. It was quiet. Too quiet. He laid a ready hand on his sword hilt. Glancing along the deck, he saw Beth keeping watch near the foremast. He wished she hadn't insisted on coming. He could handle himself against any man. Indeed, his reputation caused many to tremble in his presence. But this was no place for a woman. Then suddenly, he saw movement behind her. Three men armed with cutlasses and daggers came rushing up the fore-hatchway. All of them were six – no, make that seven – feet tall, with scarred faces and powerful builds. Strangely, one resembled Arthur Jones, while the other two were identical to a couple of schoolmasters he had particularly hated…

"Beth!" he cried. Calculating that by the time he had

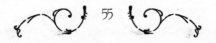

55

run the length of the main deck it would be too late, John pulled out his sword and cut through one of the mainstay ropes and used it to swing towards the attackers.

"John!" Beth swooned. "Only you can save me now!"

She screamed as the biggest of the villains – who must have been more than eight feet tall actually, with arms as big as tree trunks – swept Beth off her feet and held her above his head like a trophy.

"Captain Jack Turner of the Revenge at your service!" he cried and, like a swooping hawk, John struck the man down as he swung past. Then he let go of the rope and performed a somersault over the head of another man, landing perfectly on…

"I said, PAY ATTENTION, TURNER!"

John came to his senses with such a start that he only just managed to catch the edge of his desk to stop himself falling off his chair. Thomas Rutherford, the sour-faced Chief of Clerks, stood over him.

"Sir?"

"The accounts for the provisioning of the *Lion*. Are they ready yet? Mister Jones wishes to see them."

"Very nearly, sir. I'm working on them right now."

Rutherford peered down at John's desk. "That looks more like a playbill to me, lad."

John hastily covered Beth's leaflet with some more official documents. "Uh, no sir. The figures will be ready in ten minutes!"

Once he was alone again, John pulled the playbill back out. He realized that while he he'd been daydreaming, he had scrawled the name *Doodgaan* next to the engraving of Beth Johnson in full costume. What did the word mean, in any case? Where was it from? And what would Beth think of him if she knew he had left his friend alone on that horrible, ghostly ship? Had Arthur Jones even done anything about it yet? John chewed his lip. It had been hours since he had gone to see his senior officer and yet there was still no word of Will. A girl like Beth would only be impressed by a man of action – and that's exactly what John was. Or could be, if he put his mind to it.

He made his decision. He would go back to Mr Jones and ask – no, *demand* – that something be done immediately to rescue his friend. After hurriedly completing the paperwork for the *Lion*, he took it over to Rutherford's desk.

"I'll take the accounts up to Mister Jones's office, shall I, sir? Save you the trouble."

"You will? Oh, very well," Rutherford replied curtly. "And quick about it. We've already kept him waiting

long enough."

Clutching the accounts, John made his way back up to the top floor of the building. His nerve faltered somewhat as he stood before that great oak door again, but he was boosted by imagining Beth was watching him, impressed by his bold move. He knocked firmly. There was no reply, but the door had not been closed properly and it swung open as soon as his knuckles made contact, revealing an apparently empty office. John pulled back for a moment and checked that the corridor was clear, trying all the time to bring his nerves under control. He would leave the accounts on Jones's desk and come back again later to enquire about Will. He took a cautious step inside, then a couple more.

The sight that met his eyes stopped him dead in his tracks.

Arthur Jones's chair lay on the floor on its side. Papers from his desk were strewn around it, splashed with black ink from an upturned inkpot and red ink from … John felt his heart begin to thump against his ribs. He walked over to the desk and took a closer look at the papers. That wasn't red ink. It was blood! It was splattered all over the table and the papers, forming a trail across the floor. John dropped his accounts down onto the desk.

 58

What on earth had happened here?

The bloody trail led to a door at the back of the room. He had no idea what – or who – was on the other side, but he knew that he ought to investigate. Something very bad had surely happened here and he couldn't just walk away and do nothing, however much he might want to. John followed the blood trail right to the door and turned the handle. It opened onto a narrow, dimly lit passageway. Taking a deep breath, he set off into the shadowy corridor, where he could just make out the trail of vivid red splats going all the way along the passageway and round a corner. They looked like circular warning signs surrounded by crimson exclamation marks that spoke of danger. It was only when the trail came to an end that John looked up.

What he saw made his heart stop.

The blood traces had brought him back out onto the furthest end of the main corridor on the top floor; to an area of the Navy Board offices that John had seen from a distance many times, but never dared set foot in. He was right outside the huge double doors to the office of the Navy Commissioner, Sir Roger Fortescue himself. John studied the floor to make sure he hadn't been mistaken. But the trail of blood continued underneath the doors

and into the commissioner's office. He glanced anxiously back along the corridor. There wasn't a soul in sight, but from within the room he heard the soft low murmur of voices. As carefully as he could, John crouched down, leaned against the door and squinted through the keyhole, trying to ignore the loud thud of his own heart.

It took his eyes a few seconds to adjust to the narrow view, but once he pressed it closer he could just make out the portly figure of the Commissioner. "It has all been taken care of," John heard him saying, with his usual unhealthy wheeze.

"And what of the ship?" another man barked in a harsh, rasping voice.

Taking great care not to make a sound, John shifted his head slightly to try and see the rest of the room. The last speaker, a squat, swarthy man, strode into view. He was wiping a large knife on a cloth that he then threw carelessly to the floor. It was covered with red smears and blotches. John saw that the middle finger on man's his left hand was missing and he shuddered, trying to keep his breathing under control.

"She has been secured at Tower Wharf. I have seen to it that everyone thinks she is simply a cargo ship adrift from her moorings," Sir Roger Fortescue replied.

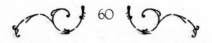

"And the boy who was caught on board?" Coming from somewhere out of John's sight, this was a different voice, one with a smooth, silky quality of authority.

John tensed. He must be talking about Will!

"Fear not. He shall not vex us any further!" croaked the swarthy man, with a malevolent chuckle that pierced John's heart.

But the unseen person with the silky voice wasn't satisfied yet. "Was there not another boy?"

John flinched, and had to force himself not to turn and run.

"Indeed. Jones kindly described him to me before I … dealt with him!" the swarthy man replied. "His name is John Turner. I shall take care of him next."

Take care of him? John gulped. What, exactly, might that entail? And what had they done with Will?

Then the shady character with the ugly voice began to walk across the room, and what John saw behind him turned his blood to ice.

The body of Arthur Jones, head flopped forward, skin grey and lifeless, was tied to a chair by the window. The front of his white shirt was crimson with fresh blood, still oozing from a gaping wound to his throat. John instinctively raised a hand to his mouth to stifle a gasp,

but in doing so caught the doorknob sharply with his knuckles. There was a loud metallic clank and the voices in the room instantly fell silent.

Blind panic flooded his mind and John stood frozen to the spot as the door flew open. For a split second he was face to face with the swarthy man with the missing finger.

"Well, well, well," the man rasped, an evil smirk playing upon his thin lips. "What have we here?"

John let out a little cry of horror, then spun round and ran for all he was worth. The last thing he heard as he skidded round the corner and flew headlong for the stairs was the pounding of heavy footsteps behind him and the squat man's evil voice calling out.

"It *was* him – the Turner boy! I shall have him, by God!"

Chapter Six

Spycraft

Making her way along Fleet Street from the Navy Board back to the Peacock and Pie, Beth stopped abruptly. It looked for all the world as though she was fascinated by a shop selling pewter plates from a counter in its open frontage. Actually, she had absolutely no interest in looking at or buying any plates. This was a test.

Beth suspected she was being followed.

Alan Strange, her spymaster, had taught her well, so she was confident she knew exactly what to do in such a situation. She had noticed a figure strolling along about twenty yards behind her when she had crossed Crutched

Friars after leaving John Turner's offices. The character was still exactly the same distance behind her when she had walked past the Tower, so she'd then deliberately turned into an alleyway off Fenchurch Street and done a full circle round the houses until she had turned back on herself to resume her journey along Fenchurch Street.

Only someone following her would have done the same pointless thing – and the sneaky so-and-so was still there. She could hear his footsteps on the cobbles, and out of the corner of her eye she kept catching a glimpse of his dark outline. Was that the gleam of an earring she saw in his ear? She restrained herself from turning back to take a proper look. It was all a matter of spycraft – Beth knew you never made it obvious that you suspected you were being followed. But from her surreptitious glances, she could tell that he wasn't old, and not very tall – perhaps even shorter than she was, although she always felt a little bit awkward about her impressive height.

Always worth noting the suspect's appearance, she told herself. It was almost fun, actually getting to use her spy skills…

Pausing at the pewter shop was a final experiment, to see whether he would stop too, or keep on walking.

Beth began to sort through a few pans and plates as if considering buying something, but all the time, and without turning her head, she was looking back down the street at the edge of her vision, trying to keep her breathing steady. The figure didn't stop, but kept walking in her direction, and the back of her neck tingled as she heard him pass right behind her. It suddenly struck her that he might not just be someone sent to follow her – but to kill her. It would only take one thrust of a long-bladed knife drawn from under his cloak and she would be finished. Perhaps it wasn't such fun after all…

She felt her shoulders tense as the footsteps faltered for a second right behind her back. All her senses were alert and highly tuned, and she was ready to spring into action in an instant. There was a pause in the youth's movement, then a scrape and a shuffle close to her back. She quickly put down the plate she was holding, ready to spin round, but it was too soon to show her hand yet. She knew she had to keep her nerve.

Then the footsteps resumed. Beth finally relaxed and let out a long breath, watching the back of the figure as he made his way up Fleet Street. She was right – he did have a big gold earring dangling from his right lobe, and she could see now that he walked with a strange, rolling

gait. Either she had been wrong about him following her and it had all been a coincidence, or this young man was very good at his job and realized if he stopped he would give himself away. Beth had a sneaking feeling that this wasn't the last she would see of the mysterious character.

Exhaling and pulling her cloak round her, she continued her journey quickly now, along wide and busy Cheapside with its many fashionable shops and noisy food market, then past St Paul's where she had received her latest mission from Alan Strange only hours before. Then finally she was back on Drury Lane and her home at the Peacock and Pie.

"Beth!" cried Maisie upon her arrival, her blue eyes shining out from a cloud of flour dust. "I'm helping Moll to make pies for the King's bonfire feast tomorrow!"

Beth laughed, finally shaking off the tension of her suspicions of being followed. "So I see!"

"At last, young lady," said Big Moll as she kneaded a large lump of dough with her great fists. "Methought the food I saved for you was going to spoil. It's there by the hearth." She turned to Maisie. "You've been very helpful, young 'un, but I can manage this now. You can go and join your friend if you like."

Beth and Maisie settled down by the gently glowing

fire, and while Beth ate, Maisie brushed the flour from her dress and jabbered excitedly about tomorrow's great feast. It would be her first Fifth of November celebration since she had arrived from America.

"…And they say half of London will be there! Lords and commoners, all manner of people. I think it might be a chance for us to try and find out some news of my father, or at least any of the White family south of the river!"

"We can, Maisie, but don't build your hopes up too much…"

"But I know there has to be a chance we can find him. I know it seems near impossible but I just … I can't explain it, Beth, but I *know* I shall find him, no matter how long it takes. Mother told me he was a good man, and it was he who chose my name before she was sent away with me inside her." She looked over at Beth with shining, hopeful eyes. "I am sure of it! We shall meet a man in Southwark who knows a man who knows a woman who knows my uncle, and he shall get a message to my father. And when we finally meet, I shall throw my arms round him and smother him in kisses and he will cry 'Why, it's Maisie White!', and I shall say—"

Beth chuckled and held up her hands, though she

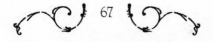

feared a little for her friend's hopefulness. "*Maisie!* I truly believe we can find him too, but you mustn't get so carried away or you will be broken-hearted if things don't work out."

Maisie smiled and said no more, but Beth could see she was still embracing her father in her daydream.

Finishing the last of her meal, Beth wiped her mouth with her napkin. "Come, Maisie. 'Tis almost time to go to the King's Theatre for the evening performance. We ought to get changed."

Maisie's eyes lit up. "And a *brand-new* play: new costumes, new scenery, new pretend people! I do so find it exciting, Beth. When I'm not selling oranges I love to watch how it's done. I don't know how you remember all those words! But do you think one day *I* could be in a play?"

Beth grinned at the young girl, thinking again how alike they were. She too had ambitions. William Huntingdon was a fine manager, but she had her own vision of how a theatre could be run – including having far more actresses than anyone did at present.

"I'm sure you could, Maisie!" she said encouragingly.

Daylight had faded as they left the tavern and set off on the short journey down Drury Lane. The lane itself

was broad and neat at one end with many fine houses, but narrowed at the other, with several shady lanes of dubious repute running off it. Beth helped Maisie to carry some of her great load of oranges in a basket, and as they walked she decided to try her lines out on her young friend.

"Thou art an unworthy rapscallion!" Beth declared dramatically.

Maisie frowned. "What's a 'rapscallion'?"

"Someone who is naughty and cheeky – like you!"

"I am not! Well, perhaps I can be a little cheeky on occasion…"

"Is thine heart so hard as to deny me my what is rightly mine?" she said, clutching her free hand to her chest.

"Oh, I would never deny you anything, Beth, you know that."

Beth chuckled. "It's just acting, Maisie!"

"I know – yet you say it so … so … *believably*," Maisie said, blushing at being caught out.

"Well, that's exactly the idea!"

They were in high spirits as they left Drury Lane and turned into the alley leading to the stage door of the theatre.

Soon after they had done so, there was a movement in the shadows behind them. From a darkened doorway, a boy with a golden earring emerged and began to follow them at a safer distance…

Chapter Seven
Pursuit

"A plague on your eyes, you little cur. Wait 'til I gets hold of yer!"

John ran on, ignoring the angry cries of the portly gentleman he had sent tumbling into a pie-man, and barely even registering the curses of the poor street vendor himself, now sprawling on the ground with his tray and his food all around him on the filthy cobbles. John was a well-mannered young man, who would not usually behave in such a way. Then again, he was not usually being chased through the streets by murderous villains like these two, that the man with the missing

finger had sent after him. Captain Jack Turner of the *Revenge* would not let a fat oaf nor a tray of pies get in his way. Captain Jack would not be running away in the first place, come to think of it ... but John decided he could worry about that some other time.

He had been heading towards his house in Shadwell, but as he left the messy scene behind and forced himself on, leg muscles burning and lungs heaving fit to burst, it dawned on him that his pursuers might know – or could easily find out – where he lived.

It wasn't safe, and he needed a different place to lie low.

He knew he must think fast, but where could he go? There were plenty of anonymous lanes and gloomy alleys, but many of them were dead ends where he would be caught like a rat in a trap. He dared to glance back over his shoulder. The bigger of the two henchmen was a long way behind and slowing, red-faced and gasping; but the younger and slimmer one with the evil, rat-like face was gaining on him with every stride.

This was no game – John was certain the man with the missing finger had instructed these two to slit his throat, just as he himself had done with Arthur Jones. John winced at the memory of the ugly, fatal wound to

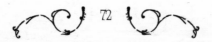

his senior officer's neck. He desperately needed a place to hide.

But then, just like that, he spotted the solution.

On the side of a derelict house on Jewry Street there was a poster whose design and wording he instantly recognized: it was a larger version of the playbill Beth Johnson had given him. He remembered suddenly that he had in his pocket a personal invitation to the play from London's leading actress. The King's Theatre would be his refuge! John fished for it in his pocket ... but it was not there.

Panicking, he dipped into his other pockets as he ran, checking them all twice, three times each. The playbill signed by Beth had gone, along with his chance of being shown backstage to meet her. It must have fallen out during the chase. He cursed to himself, but decided that the theatre would still make a good refuge. John nipped down an alley he knew led out onto Fenchurch Street, and headed west.

He felt a tremendous sense of relief when he saw the theatre ahead of him, but instead of going directly in he veered into an alley and paused for a moment, leaning with his back to the wall while he tried to get his breath back. His legs trembled, and there was a sharp,

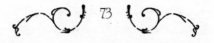

acid taste in his mouth and throat. After a few seconds, he cautiously peered round the end of the side street, back in the direction he had come. There was no sign of the two villains. He gave it a couple more minutes, straightened out his doublet and cloak, smoothed his windswept, sweat-dampened hair and strolled into the theatre trying to look as casual as possible. Luckily he had enough money for a seat and a bite to eat, so feeling in need of something to replenish his energy he went in search of a fruit-seller as soon as he was inside.

At the back of the theatre he saw a few people gathered round a young orange-seller: a pretty young girl with shiny brown hair in ringlets and bright blue, canny eyes. John joined the back of the queue and waited patiently to be served. His attention wandered around the theatre, a place he had never visited in his life before.

It was an impressive sight – a tall building with several tiers of seats, slowly beginning to fill up now. The wealthy in their finery were down in the pit and up in the boxes, and the commoner folk high in the upper gallery, gazing down and squawking excitedly like starlings on a clothes line. The stage itself was magnificent, with enormous arches either side that seemed to belong to some grand building of ancient Rome. Above the stage ornately carved figures flanked the royal coat of arms, all picked out in scarlet and gold and glittering in the candlelight. John's eyes glazed over as he imagined the deep blue velvet-looking curtains pulling back and Beth Johnson striding across the stage towards the audience...

Then he heard a voice that made him freeze.

"I'll take two of your juiciest oranges, my dear..." The man was trying to sound friendly enough, but it was a cruel, rasping tone – one that John had heard before. Then the man reached out to offer his money, and John saw the short stub where the middle finger of his left hand should have been.

How could the villain possibly have tracked him down here? John was sure he had given the man's two chasing henchmen the slip, and London was one of the biggest, busiest cities in the world. He could have been anywhere by now. Why on earth was the fingerless man here now?

He quickly slipped away from the queue before the man could turn round, and found a seat behind the tallest person he could see, hunching up his shoulders and sinking as low into the shadows as possible.

Chapter Eight
Turning the Tables

Beth took a deep breath to steady herself. No matter how many plays she performed in, nor how popular she became, she always felt like this just before the curtain was about to open. Her legs felt unsteady, there was a queasiness in her stomach, and she had to fight off the old fear that she would forget her lines and the cast and the whole audience would be staring at her in silence, waiting for her to say something. She rubbed her cheeks vigorously with her hands and reminded herself that she had learned her lines well, that everything had gone really smoothly in rehearsal. It worked. Her nerves began to settle, and she could finally enjoy looking forward to entertaining the gathering audience. That was, until she heard the whining tones of Benjamin Lovett behind her.

"It vexes me so to see how much make-up that *child* wears! And did you see how gaudily it is applied? She looks like a—"

Beth marched right up to Lovett. "Too much make-up? Well then, sir, I had better get rid of some!"

She planted a big kiss on his forehead, leaving a large crimson imprint of her lips slap in the middle. Lovett spluttered indignantly, and the actors standing nearby burst into laughter, but this was quickly cut short by William Huntingdon, the theatre manager.

"Hush, now! One minute 'til curtain up – to your positions, and good luck, everyone!"

As soon as the curtain had risen and the play was under way, Beth forgot her nerves completely and began to relish her role as Henry, soon to be revealed as Henrietta. But Lovett, whom she played opposite in most of her scenes, had a worrying, self-satisfied smirk on his face tonight which was beginning to make Beth feel edgy.

Perhaps she should never have given him that kiss. She knew what he was like, and she guessed he was planning his revenge.

In the play, Lovett's evil character wants to marry Beth's sister. There was a scene where Beth – as Henry – embraces and kisses her sister on the cheek. Lovett's character thinks this proves they are lovers, and attacks. However, William Huntingdon had been so impressed by Beth's spirited swordplay during rehearsals, and was so sure that the audience would love it too, that he had changed this scene completely. In the new version, *Beth* was to win the fight, and she couldn't wait to play the scene!

However, she suspected that if Lovett was going to try anything, it would be now. He was nothing if not predictable, and she wouldn't put it past him to try and turn the tables yet again and get the better of her. But considering how easily Beth had beaten him on the previous occasion, she was not unduly worried.

Not until, that was, she discovered *how* he planned to defeat her...

"Unhand that maiden, thou cursed varlet!"

When Lovett bounded in to confront her and drew his sword, she immediately saw that it was not a flimsy stage

prop like the one she had, but a real duelling broadsword with a powerful steel blade and a razor-sharp cutting edge. She heard gasps from the actors in the wings.

"'Tis wealth and property you seek and naught else! Thou hast no love for this woman!" he cried.

Drawing her weapon, Beth's eyes widened and she felt the blood coursing through her veins. She knew Lovett wouldn't try to injure her; he simply wanted to destroy her narrow, fragile blade and declare himself the champion, getting back to the way the script had been written in the first place. The trouble was, he was as clumsy as he was pompous. If she wasn't careful, she could easily imagine him running her through by mistake. Yet how could she parry his blows when one strike from his sword would cut hers in two as if it were made of matchsticks?

"'Tis a love none can thwart, thou treacherous creature!"

He was hamming things up for all he was worth, and Lovett now edged towards her in fighting stance. Beth began to back up, but she soon felt scenery at her back blocking her retreat. He raised his sword and struck at her, his face red with ire and the veins in his neck standing out with the effort. Beth quickly swayed to one side and felt the broad blade whistle past her face and

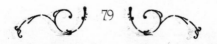

79

brush the shoulder of her costume.

"Thou shall marry her over my dead body!" she shouted and made a lunge with her own sword, and although it had a blunted end, the poke in his stomach was still enough to make Lovett yelp and jump back. There were titters from the audience, but this only served to enrage him further.

"Ha! Then let it be so!"

He came at her like a charging bull, but this was just what Beth had been expecting. She faked a move to his left, causing him to jab in that direction with his sword, but then launched into a forward roll to the right of him. She finished the movement by coming up onto her feet right behind him, and swished at the belt encircling his enormous belly, which held his breeches in place. She then lightly skipped backwards to give herself room, and as he lumbered after her, his breeches slithered down to his knees, causing him to stumble, finally ending up around his ankles. He crashed to the stage in a cloud of dust and with a loud groan, where he floundered helplessly like a beached whale.

The audience roared with laughter, and there were cheers as Beth placed one foot lightly on his back and raised her sword aloft with one hand, while whisking off her cloak with the other to reveal women's clothes below.

"I, Henrietta, sister of Isabella, declare myself her champion!"

As Beth basked in the applause, she caught sight of a familiar pair of eyes in the audience. He was ducking down behind a beanpole of a man, but there was no doubting it was John Turner from the Navy Board – perhaps he was going to take her up on her invitation to come backstage? Her mind clicked back into spy mode and she tried to catch his eye, but he seemed more interested in scanning the faces in the audience around him than looking at the stage. In fact, the poor boy looked terrified of something. But what? Just as she was returning her attentions to the stage, another young figure attracted her gaze. Standing in the shadows in the far corner was the silhouette of a youth with a distinctive glint of an earring in one ear. She couldn't see his features, but she knew he was staring back at her.

So she hadn't shaken him off.

He was good. Very good. But what was he doing here? And why was he so interested in her?

Chapter Nine

Stage-struck

John tried to look out of the corner of his eye without turning his head and making it obvious that he was aware he was being sought. He had spotted that the man with the missing finger was on the prowl, like a black shadow in the darkness of the auditorium, stalking up and down the aisles, scanning the rows of faces. As he drew ever nearer, John, who was about six seats from the aisle, leaned forwards so that he was hidden by the tall man in front of him. But soon his hunter would be level with him, and that ploy would not be enough. The audience was currently so captivated by a tender scene involving Beth and the girl playing her sister that the earlier noisy enthusiasm had settled into a sympathetic silence, and John could just detect the rasping breath of his tracker as he climbed the last step that would bring him onto his row. At the last second, John bent down as if to adjust the buckle on his boot. As he did so he turned and got an upside-down view of the swarthy man lifting his foot as if to move on – but then pausing, like a cat stalking a mouse he knows is hiding somewhere close by. How long could John remain in this bent-over position without it being obvious that he was trying to avoid being seen? He played with his buckle, he tugged at his heel as if the boot was uncomfortable, he silently prayed…

At last, the man continued on, breathing huskily, searching; John felt as though he could breathe again. He slowly straightened up, still looking at the man with the missing finger, and he saw a piece of paper sticking out of the man's pocket. John immediately recognized the feminine handwriting scrawled on it. It was the playbill Beth had given to him. One of his pursuers must have found it during the chase and handed it to their chief.

Even though he hadn't been spotted this time, John knew he was a sitting duck. His hunter clearly wasn't

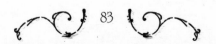

the sort to give up and would continue searching 'til he had cornered his quarry. So as soon as he had gone a couple of steps further, John slipped out of his seat and quietly crept away in the opposite direction. He moved to the far side of the theatre where there was another exit, hastening more and more the further he got from his tracker. But what he saw at this exit brought him to a sudden halt.

It was one of the men who had been chasing him through the streets. There wasn't enough light to see his face, but John would have recognized his outline anywhere, and knew it was the bigger of the two men. He glanced across to the other exit, and the smaller, rat-faced accomplice guarded that one too. He was trapped. All they had to do was wait 'til the play had finished and everyone began to leave.

John crouched down in the aisle to give himself thinking time. What would Captain Jack Turner of the *Revenge* do now? Probably cut a rope holding the scenery up, swing across the stage into the wings and out through a back door. But that might not go too well with the theatre-goers – not to mention Beth, who seemed to be building up to the climax of the play judging from the drama on stage and the increasing clamour of the audience, who were crying out her character's name and encouraging her to overcome the villain. He had just come back on stage and was being booed and hissed every time he spoke.

In crouching down, John was now at eye level with one of the few spare seats in the house. On that seat, a man had placed his cloak and hat. The hat was a large one with a broad, floppy brim, and the man was totally engrossed in the play: shouting, clapping, booing. And the hat and cloak were both within reach...

John quickly discovered that the hat was much too big for him – which was a good thing, because it almost came down over his eyes. The wide brim, together with the high collar of the cloak, did the rest of the work, casting his face in deep shadow. Captain Jack, in addition to being a swashbuckling naval hero, was a master of disguise. Well, he hadn't been 'til now, but still ... The henchmen would be looking for a young, upright man, so John added to his masquerade by stooping and shuffling along stiffly in the hope that it made him look much older.

With his head down, he lumbered towards the exit guarded by the bigger man. But he had picked the wrong moment. Someone was coming his way and instinct told

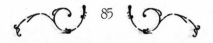

him it was the man with the missing finger. John veered away from the exit and found himself walking towards the girl with the tray of oranges. She was standing with her back to a wall at the side of the theatre, and as he approached she held one out for him and began to say something, but he ignored her and walked on, positioning himself behind her. If he kept low and in her shadow, perhaps…

But it was too late for that. They were coming his way, and if they got much closer they would surely see through his disguise. Peering round the orange girl's bonnet, John saw the man with the missing finger catch the eye of the guard at the exit and nod in his direction. The big man began to move in, and the rat-faced man was also leaving his post and heading this way. It looked like his cover was already blown.

There seemed to be no escape, but Captain Jack Turner wouldn't be so easily beaten. He was clever, resourceful, and afraid of nothing. If the back of theatre was blocked off, then he would just have to leave the front way.

He set off towards the brightly lit stage with its woodland scenery and its cast in resplendent, colourful costume. But the closer he got the more he found that Captain Jack was fading rapidly from his imagination,

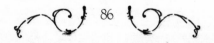

and it was shy John Turner, the lowly clerk, who was walking on rather wobbly legs towards his embarrassing fate. Reality was kicking in fast and with sickening clarity. Those were real actors being watched by a real audience, and it felt as if the whole building was closing in on him as he hovered by the edge of the stage, hesitating, gulping and feeling the sticky dryness of his throat.

There were only five steps between him and the stage now, but it looked like the tallest mountain, and his knees had turned to a quivering mush. He could hear the rasping voice close behind now, yet didn't think he could bring himself to go up there in front of all these people…

Then he heard a woman's voice calling down at him from the stage. Strangely, although his name wasn't mentioned, the proclamation definitely seemed to be aimed at him. Which was impossible – wasn't it?

"I said … EGAD! My aged Uncle George doth arrive – the wealthiest merchant in London and one who hath the ear of the King himself. He shall save us!"

Beth Johnson, the finest actress in all England, was looking down at John and holding out her hand, willing him to come up and take it. He saw her glancing briefly but urgently towards his pursuers as she waited.

Somehow, she understood what was happening! Hearing the low, conspiratorial whispers of the men getting closer, John felt himself propelled forward as if attracted by a magnet until he finally grasped Beth's slim hand. She was stronger than she looked and he allowed himself to be pulled up on stage. A murmur of intrigue rippled through the audience at this development.

Once up there, dazzled by the lights yet still able to make out the rows and rows of faces all apparently directed at him, John froze, unsure what to do next. He was no actor and his nerves and desire not to be caught by his stalkers had meant he'd hardly taken in what the play was about. Something to do with Beth dressed as a man but really being a woman, and the fat old actor Lovett's character being angry with her? Lovett had just grabbed the other actress on stage from behind and was holding a knife to her throat, saying something about how if he couldn't have her, no one would.

"You may have bested me with the sword, but now I have the prize we both covet," the portly actor cried.

As the other actress wailed pitifully and wriggled in his grasp, Beth turned to John.

"Oh, Uncle, whatever shall we do?" Seeing John's horrified look under the brim of his great hat, she nodded imperceptibly but encouragingly. The audience were waiting in silent expectation for his reply.

"Er … Well, we could … perchance … try to…" He couldn't help peering out from under his hat into the audience to see if the game was up and the man with the missing finger was racing towards him. But his enemy seemed to have been as fooled as the audience about his being a part of the play. After a brief glance, he said something to his henchmen and they began another sweep of the theatre.

"Speak up, Uncle!" Beth urged him. Lovett eyed John contemptuously and looked as if he might storm off the stage at any moment. He needed to pull himself together quickly.

"I say that we should … we might … I say that I am not your aged Uncle George, but your brother Captain Jack of His Majesty's ship Revenge!" John cried.

A cheer went up from the audience as he bounded across the stage and snatched Beth's sword from where it lay on the boards.

"My brother – my hero!" swooned Beth.

"Eh?" said Lovett.

John ran towards Lovett, dived onto his front and slid between both his and Isabella's legs, springing up behind

them and pointing his sword at Lovett's bottom.

"Oh Lord, not again…" Lovett whined.

The audience erupted into laughter, and there were cries of "Make a pin cushion of him!" and "Prod the villain good and proper!"

Lovett had finally reached breaking point. "THIS IS ALL WRONG!" he roared. "THIS CANNOT BE ALLOWED!"

"But it shall be, Alexander!" Beth countered, standing with her hands defiantly on her hips. "If you value your life – and your bottom – you shall release my sister!"

Almost drowned out by laughter, Lovett kept his grip on Isabella and his knife to her throat. "Never!"

"PROD! PROD! PROD!" came the chant from below.

So John did.

Benjamin Lovett arched his back and squealed like a pig, dropping his knife. Emboldened by the encouragement from the now near hysterical laughter and yelling from the crowd, John made a deft lunge at Lovett's hat, meaning to skewer it and throw it into the audience. If anything, he was more successful than he'd intended, because the enraged man's wig came off too, revealing a shiny pink balding head beneath. Lovett

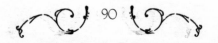

90

let go of Isabella and swivelled round to make a grab at John, but he only succeeded in getting his feet in a tangle and stumbling to the floor in an undignified heap once again. Beth grasped Isabella's hand and pulled her away from her captor, and they embraced to the delight of the audience.

"That's it, John!" she whispered over Isabella's shoulder. "Take a bow!"

She and Isabella held hands and bowed low as applause and cheers thundered around the theatre.

As the curtain began to fall and he hurried off after Beth, John heard the bewildered actress who had played Isabella talking to a stage hand:

"What on earth just happened?"

Chapter Ten

A Dilemma

Beth and John sat catching their breath in Beth's dressing room. They could hear Benjamin Lovett storming up and down outside, complaining to anyone who would listen about "that girl's" outrageous conduct and of being made a laughing stock, and, eventually, William Huntingdon's soothing tones as he tried to explain that the surprise ending of the play had gone down even better than the planned version.

Beth took one look at John peering at her from under the oversized hat he seemed to have forgotten he was still wearing, then suddenly threw her head back and laughed at the absurdity of it all.

"That was utterly ridiculous!"

John joined in her laughter, clearly seeing the funny side of it too, despite having been shaken up by the whole encounter. But he was also staring at her as if there was something else.

"Oh, I hope you don't think I was making fun of you," she said quickly.

"No, no, it's not that. I was just thinking you … you have a lovely laugh." He looked away, his face reddening.

She smiled, suddenly feeling a little shy herself, unusually. "Thank you, John."

"But I do hope I haven't ruined your career," he said.

"*Ruined* it? You've made both me and the play more popular than ever! The only problem is, if word of the new ending spreads, then the next audience will be expecting us to do it every time. Still, I expect Mister Huntingdon, our manager, can employ another actor to take your part. Not that anyone but you could make such an amazing Captain Jack of the *Revenge*!" she said with a grin. "However did you think that one up so quickly?"

"Oh, 'tis something that I…" John stopped himself and fidgeted uncomfortably in his chair. "'Tis just something that popped into my head out of nowhere."

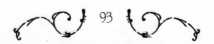

"Well then, you have a fine imagination. Perhaps acting should be your calling rather than being a clerk at the Navy Board!" She sobered, remembering her mission for Strange. Could the man following John have had something to do with it? "For now, you can remove that silly hat and provide me with an explanation. I spotted that someone was after you, but who was it? And why?"

John removed the hat and threw it onto an empty chair. It was only now that Beth remembered how handsome she had thought him when they had first met at the Navy Board. The hat had ruffled his light brown wavy hair, yet in a funny way it made him look more attractive. She blinked a little, trying to refocus in case what he told her might have some significance to the mysterious drifting ship she'd been sent to investigate.

"I hardly know where to begin," John said. "It all started this morning, when I was ordered to investigate a strange vessel adrift on the Thames with my colleague, Will Brown—"

He was interrupted by an urgent knock at the door, and Beth picked up his hat and handed it back to him. "Put it back on – at least for now," she whispered.

She called out for the visitor to enter, and was relieved to see Maisie's shining blue eyes and brown ringlets

spiralling tightly from beneath her bonnet as she peered round the door.

"There be a visitor for you, Mistress Beth."

"Who is it?"

"Don't know. A man…" She leaned closer and added in a conspiratorial whisper, "And he doesn't look very nice, if you ask me."

"I see. Well, please inform him that I'm tired after my performance and can't see anyone just yet, Maisie."

Maisie went outside with her message, but soon they heard raised voices and footsteps approaching.

"You don't understand, girl. I must see her."

"But she said—"

"Step aside, wench!"

Beth heard some scuffling and a rough, rasping voice, then saw that beneath his hat John had suddenly turned pale. He sprang from his chair and dived beneath a long clothes rail at the end of the dressing room where Beth's costumes hung. He just managed to pull his feet out of sight as the visitor entered, with Maisie pulling determinedly on his coat tail to try to keep him out.

"I told him 'no', Mistress Beth," she grunted, "but he wouldn't listen!"

Beth stood up indignantly. "It's all right, Maisie. Let

95

us discover from this man how it is he thinks fit to enter my private room without consent."

She watched the intruder's face to see how he reacted to her words. He was short and stocky, with dark, greasy hair hanging limply beneath his hat. The faintest of sneers had played across his lips when he first heard Beth comment on his intrusion – but he managed to quickly twist it into the nearest thing to a smile he was probably capable of.

"A thousand apologies, madam," he said, removing his hat and bowing. "It brings great shame upon me to invade the privacy of so talented and famous a member of the fair sex, and I humbly beseech your forgiveness." He bowed again, even lower this time – but he could disguise neither the cruel undertone to his voice nor the faint glimmer of contempt behind his eyes.

"Say your piece, then leave, if you please, sir."

The man gestured towards Maisie, who stood scowling at him, tensed as if ready to launch herself if he so much as laid a finger on her friend, and Beth noticed that the middle finger of his left hand was just a short, scarred stump. "T'would be better if we might converse in private, mistress…"

"Maisie is as a sister to me, sir. There is nothing I may

hear that she may not."

"Very well. My name is Edmund Groby, and I am here to warn you that a young man by the name of John Turner of the Navy Board may have a design to take your life."

Pride almost prevented Beth from admitting it, but now she knew this *was* something she didn't want Maisie to be involved in. "Uh, Maisie, perhaps this *gentleman* was right. I'm going to get someone to take you home."

"But I can't leave you, Mistress Beth – not now!"

"I shall be perfectly safe. Please trust me, and go home to Moll."

"But he said someone may have a design to take your life? What if this murderer should succeed! You are the only friend I have in the world—!"

"Hush, hush," Beth said quickly, glancing crossly at Groby. "We do not know for certain what he says is true," she said quietly to Maisie. "Remember our sword fight? You know I am very capable of taking care of myself. Do not worry."

Despite Maisie's further protestations, Beth went to her dressing-room door and swiftly summoned old Matthew the prompter to escort her friend back to the Peacock and Pie.

97

This mysterious visitor and his news about John had put her mind into a whirl. It seemed very unlikely indeed, but spies lurked anywhere, as she well knew. She returned to Groby, determined to appear outwardly composed.

"Who has sent you, sir?"

His eyes, sunk deep inside his sullen face, twitched from side to side shiftily. "That I am not at liberty to reveal, mistress. But may I ask you to take a look at this? It comes from the young man I am trying to trace. You will see he has written a very short message on it."

He withdrew from his pocket what Beth could instantly see was a playbill for tonight's performance. Looking closer at it, she saw that next to the engraving of her in her "Henrietta" costume was a single word written in a spidery hand:

Doodgaan

"What is that word?" she asked Groby. "An anagram?"

"Nay, Mistress. 'Tis from the Dutch tongue."

"And what, pray, does it mean?"

"It means *to die*, *to perish*. It means *death*. He could well be a traitor for the enemy."

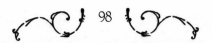

Beth stared at the piece of paper with the ominous word scrawled right next to her image, which this stranger claimed was written by John, trying not to betray her confusion. This man might be coarse and unpleasant, but that did not mean he was not telling the truth. She had given John just such a playbill. If Mr Groby's story were false, then was it mere coincidence that John had scribbled "Die" by her picture? Might he really be a spy for the Dutch, with whom England might soon be at war? Sir Alan Strange had always taught her that there was no such thing in this business as a coincidence, and he had, after all, sent her to the Navy Board to investigate the drifting ship. Perhaps it had all been a ploy of some sort – a dangerous one at that – to draw an enemy out? She wouldn't put it past the spymaster.

She glanced in the direction of the costume rail. Clearing her throat, she looked the unpleasant man in the eye.

"Mister Groby, there is something you ought to know…"

Chapter Eleven
The Golden Earring

The sneering smile returned to Edmund Groby's face.

"What is it you have to say, my dear?"

"'Tis about John Turner … I do believe your story, Mister Groby – and a man I believe was John Turner has visited me." At the edge of her vision Beth noticed some of the costumes on the rail move slightly. Was John going to make a run for it?

"Very good, Mistress Johnson. I knew you would see sense! Whither can he be found?"

"Much closer than you think," she said slowly. There was a distinct ripple of cotton and silk on the clothes rail

this time, but Groby was focusing so intently on Beth in his eagerness for the information that he failed to notice.

"Pray go on, mistress!"

"Well, I last saw the man I believe was John Turner under a pile of clothes ... in an alley off Drury Lane. He *did* try to kill me – he jumped out of the alley and drew a dagger when I was on my way to rehearsal. Fortunately, my stage training allowed me to evade him, and a swift blow with a nearby brick sent him flying, though it was indeed a close-run thing. But I am something of a skilled fighter myself, sir. He was unconscious when I left him, prostrate under a mound of abandoned garments." She smiled proudly and, she hoped, convincingly, to drive her story home.

Groby's eyes bore into Beth's own, and she couldn't tell whether he believed her or not. She certainly didn't believe *him*. His story about John and the playbill had thrown her into confusion for a moment, but she simply couldn't see John as a spy – and certainly not a murderer. If he intended to kill her, why would he not have done so when they were alone?

Groby frowned. "Hmm ... When did this incident happen?" He took a step closer to her.

Beth shrugged. "I can't remember exactly. As I say, it

was just before I reached the theatre."

Groby came closer still. She could hear his breath rasping in his throat and smell its foulness as his face loomed nearer to hers.

"I should have thought that such an event would be permanently engraved in one's memory – that the time of it would be impossible to forget. Yet you seem unusually vague, Mistress Johnson…" He put a hand on her shoulder in an outwardly friendly way, but his grip was powerful and pressed muscle against bone painfully.

Beth refused to flinch and eyed him boldly. "Sir, I have told you all I know. Now I must ask you to leave my dressing room."

He kept a firm grip on her, his fingertips digging into her flesh like a vice. It felt as if he were strong enough to pick her up with that one hand and throw her across the room like a rag doll. "Pray delve a little deeper into your memory, mistress, and see if you can come up with the true facts."

"I have *told* you the true facts. Remove your hand, you—"

"John Turner was seen not an hour ago. You are lying!"

He yanked her towards him and raised his other hand – the one with the missing finger – towards her throat.

 102

But just at that moment, her dressing-room door burst open and Groby hastily let go of her and backed off.

They both turned to see a strange, shabby figure amble into the room, and Beth saw that it was the boy with the golden earring who had been following her earlier. His face had an unwashed, weatherworn look and it was hard to judge just how old he was, but he was at least a year or two older than her. Beth's heart sank – was he Groby's accomplice?

But instead the young man began shouting: "Come and see! Soldiers from the Tower all over the place! People say they're looking for a traitor to the King!"

Edmund Groby's eyes widened and he opened his mouth as if to speak – but then he suddenly rushed for the door. The newcomer quickly tried to get out of the way, but clumsily stumbled into Groby as he passed. The older man pushed him roughly away and disappeared.

The look of innocent excitement on the boy's face quickly transformed into a knowing grin. "Blimey, he scarpered a bit sharpish didn't he? Almost as if he'd got something to fear from soldiers after a traitor. There ain't any soldiers, by the way – just in case you were wondering. Thought it would give us time to get away."

There was a distinctly shifty look to his worldly blue

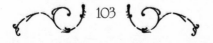

103

eyes, and Beth rounded on him. "What *I'm* wondering is why people keep invading my dressing room – not to mention why you were following me on my way here!"

"Temper, temper! If I'd known you was going to be so ungrateful I might have left you to manage on your own against that ugly feller."

"But how did you know I was in danger from him?"

The boy with the gold earring was still smiling, enjoying her puzzlement. "I'm your guardian angel, me!"

"How can I trust you any more than I could that Edmund Groby? And if you don't give me a straight answer this time I'll shove my boot so far up your—"

"All right, all right! Perhaps I'm not an angel." He held out a slightly grubby hand. "I'm Ralph Chandler at your service, that's who I am. And although few would describe me as angelic – especially the judges and juries in most of the boroughs of London – perhaps you will trust me better if I mention one word: *Alan Strange*."

Beth stared at his hand and back up to him, her heart suddenly beating faster.

"Er ... I hate to interrupt, but that's two words," came a muffled voice from beneath the rail of theatrical costumes.

Beth turned quickly towards the clothes rail. "Oh! In

all the excitement I quite forgot you were there!" She rushed to help John out from his hiding place.

"He does look easily forgettable, to be fair," Ralph commented as he saw the bedraggled figure emerge with a feather from one of the costumes stuck in his hair. "And I never learned me numbers: two words, one word – it's all the same to me. But when the words are *Alan Strange* it ain't the number of 'em that matter, if you get me drift."

Beth studied him with suspicion. "You were sent by Alan Strange?"

"Taught me everything I know." He lowered his voice a little. "About spying, leastways. Picked up a few tricks on the streets meself, you might say."

Beth folded her arms and scoffed. "Well, I spotted you following me, so perhaps you need to brush up on your skills—"

"*Spying?*" John interjected. "Who *is* Alan Strange?"

Beth hesitated before replying, glancing at Ralph before she spoke. "The King has many enemies, John. You know as well as I do about the Dutch, but there are also enemies within. It is not so very long since Cromwell's Republic was overthrown and the King was returned to his rightful place at the head of our nation.

It was a turbulent time that divided the people, and there are still some who would have the old ways brought back and rid themselves of the King yet again. His Majesty is well aware of this possibility, and needed someone he could trust to keep an eye on those lurking in the shadows…"

"So Alan Strange is a spymaster?"

"Yes."

John looked from Beth to Ralph and back again. "So you two are…?"

"That's enough for one day," Ralph chipped in. "Edmund Groby will soon realize he's been fooled, and he won't be best pleased."

Beth nodded. "Quickly. Follow me. We'll leave by the back door and we can go to my lodgings until we're sure it's safe – it's not far."

"Nay," said Ralph. "They will expect you to go there. It's likely they know where you live, as a famous stage actress and all," he said with a pointed look. "They don't know me, though, me being a true spy. We ought to go to my place."

Beth pursed her lips and narrowed her eyes. "Alan Strange never mentioned you. I still only have your word that you are who you say you are."

Ralph shrugged. "Our enemies seem to know all about both of you – where you live, where you work. My hideout is safe. Your choice…"

Chapter Twelve

Culpeper's

"What *is* this place?" asked John, holding his kerchief against his nose as they made their way through the shop on Black Swan Alley where Ralph had taken them. It was a crowded, dingy place illuminated by flickering candlelight. Strange-smelling plants and herbs in pots, jars and boxes filled the shelves that lined the walls. Bottles of odorous, mud-coloured liquids bubbled on the counter beside a precarious pile of mysterious-looking, dusty, leather-bound books.

"I know," Ralph chimed. "I thought I'd come across a witch's coven the first time I set foot in here!"

A bizarre figure that had been rummaging unseen beneath the counter suddenly rose and added another book to the pile. "But now you know that it's an apothecary's shop, young Ralph," said the man in a gruff but not unfriendly voice. "Herbs and healing, that's what I do."

Beth had never seen such a remarkable sight as this tall, fiery-eyed man in black robes. He wore a scarlet cap with strange symbols embroidered all round it in silver, and masses of snowy-white hair that protruded from beneath it and fell over his shoulders. He had a matching beard that was long and bushy enough to hide a bird's nest in.

"Meet Mister Culpeper, me landlord." Ralph announced. "Just brought a few friends round for a natter, Mister C."

The unusual man's gaze lingered on Beth and John for a moment. "Yes, I'm sure you have," he said, as if used to his tenant's secretive ways.

Ralph led them to the back of the shop and up a stairway to a small, plain, sparsely furnished chamber above the shop. There was a little wooden bed with a straw mattress and a couple of blankets, a rickety chair beside it with some crumpled clothes piled on it, and an ancient wooden chest in one corner.

"As long as I behave and pay me rent, he don't ask no questions," said Ralph breezily. "Old Walter don't tell folk who it is lives here, and neither do I. You're in what the sailors call a safe haven."

"Have you been to sea, then?" John asked him curiously.

Beth looked at Ralph's hands, noticing they were rough and strong. "Yes, your earring – does that mean you were a sailor?"

"Might have visited a few far-off places, relieved a few merchantmen of a few of their wines and silks…" Ralph said shiftily.

"You were a *pirate*!" John cried with dismay.

"An *adventurer* of the high seas!" he replied indignantly. "Anyways, why don't you two perch on me bed and I'll take the chair. Only, one of the legs is dodgy and you have to sit on it just right or it has a tendency to pitch you on your bum … *Oops!* Ladies present, pardon my language."

Baffled that this young man could really also be a spy, Beth settled herself on the edge of the bed alongside John. It felt hard and uncomfortable. "I still want to know about you and Alan Strange. Why didn't he tell

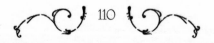

me about you?"

"Mister Strange only gives away what he needs to."

That much was true. But even an enemy who knew Strange would know that. "Whither do you meet him? What secret signal does he use to call you to him?"

"Well now, mistress, it wouldn't hardly be a secret if I went telling all and sundry, would it?"

Beth shook her head, exasperated. "Well, why did he take you into his confidence in the first place?"

For the first time, Ralph looked distinctly uncomfortable. "He got me out of a tight spot, and in return … let's just say I'm repaying a debt."

Beth hardly knew any more than she had before she had begun quizzing him, but she sensed further questions would get her nowhere, so she turned to John.

"And what is your place in all this? Why is Edmund Groby after you?"

John took a deep, shaky breath before he answered. Beth – and Ralph, if the story he told was true – had some experience of these situations, but she noticed poor John still looked rather shaken after the events of the last few hours.

"Before you visited me at the Navy Board offices this morning, I was sent with another clerk, my friend Will,

to investigate a strange ship that had turned up in the Thames," he said. "As far as we could see, there was no crew on board…"

As he continued with his tale about his friend's unearthly scream and the disappearance of the ship, Beth was reminded of Strange's words when she had showed her disappointment at being asked to solve the mystery of a mere empty ship. He had said "*apparently* empty", as if there was more to it than she had initially suspected. Now it seemed he was right.

"… and then I was knocked out," John finished.

"By *pirates*?" Ralph asked, perking up.

"Er…" began John, remembering the grappling hook he had been tugging hurtling towards his head. "Possibly. *Probably*. Anyway, when I came to, both Will and the ship had gone."

"What was her name?" Beth asked.

"*Doodgaan*."

"Ah! The name you wrote on the playbill next to my picture! Groby tried to twist it – he told me it meant you were out to kill me." She frowned. "A ship named for death…?"

"I only wrote the word next to your name because I was thinking of you…" He quickly reddened as soon

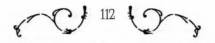

112

as he realized what he had said. "I mean, I was thinking about the ship just after you had left and given me the playbill…"

Ralph sniggered, but Beth ignored him. "I was sent to find out about that ship by Mister Strange," she said. "John, it's important that you tell me all you know about it."

"Well, when I visited the commissioner of the Navy Board later on to see whether there was any news of Will or the ship, I came upon a terrible sight…"

He went on to tell the rest of his gruesome tale: the trail of blood inside the Navy Board offices; his glimpse of Arthur Jones, his senior officer, with his throat cut, and Sir Roger Fortescue, the commissioner – who seemed to be in league with the man he now knew as Edmund Groby.

"The only clue I have is that I thought I overheard Fortescue say the *Doodgaan* had been taken to Tower Wharf. But I can't be sure I'm afraid," he said, his handsome face still pale at recounting what he had witnessed.

Beth gazed out of the window into the darkness where, between the houses at the end of the street, she could see the bobbing lights of ships on the black waters of the Thames. Was the *Doodgaan* still out there? Alan

Strange had made no mention of Will being aboard, but the fate of one appeared to be tied up with the other, and she dared not report back to her spymaster until she had got to the bottom of it.

"I will help you find your friend," she said at last.

"Finally, some action!" Ralph said, brightening. "Count me in."

"I don't need your help," Beth replied curtly.

"Don't need my help? Who's provided you with a safe place to hide out, eh? Who saved you from Edmund Groby? Little Red Riding Hood?"

"I don't even really know if you are who you say you are! But if you *are* one of Alan Strange's spies, you will know as well as I do that one of the first rules he imparts is never to believe what you're told without confirming for yourself that it is the truth."

"And the next is to use your noddle and ignore the rules if it gets results." Ralph rose from his chair and reached into his tunic. For a second Beth tensed, ready to spring up and defend herself. But Ralph merely removed a piece of paper.

"I *obtained* this from Edmund Groby when he came into your dressing room!" He flourished it in front of Beth's face, but when she tried to snatch it from him

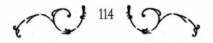

he whisked it away. "Ah! I'm not part of your team, so there's no reason why I should give you this clue to where your precious ship might be found!"

"But how did you—" John began.

Beth jumped in before Ralph could taunt them any further. "You bumped into him," she said slowly, as the realization dawned. "You pretended to stumble but … you're a pickpocket!"

"I'm a man of *many* talents that you'd find useful on your mission," he smirked. "*If* you were to dispense with your precious rules…"

"Beth, I believe him," John said. "If he had been an enemy, he could easily have led us into a trap. Instead, he got us away from Groby and even picked his pocket. I may not be a spy but I think I can tell when someone is lying, and I say Ralph is on our side."

Beth sighed, and turned to study Ralph. She knew that the best – and most dangerous – spies were the ones who were able to go along with you even to the extent of appearing to betray their own side, wheedling their way deep into your confidence 'til they had you just where they wanted you…

In her head there was a nagging doubt, but her heart told her that John was right – and that at some point they would need to call upon Ralph's Chandler's dubious skills.

"First of all, you are hardly yet a *man*," she said, then grudgingly folded her arms. "But I feel we have no choice but to trust you. All right – you're in." She stepped towards him. "But the first sign of betrayal and I cut your scrawny throat."

"Charming!" Ralph quipped, handing her the document he'd snatched from Groby.

Beth soon realized that it was a docking slip for Tower Wharf. "It looks like you were right, John," she said eagerly, glancing between the two young men and showing them the proof. "We shall all visit Tower Wharf first thing on the morrow."

"Nah!" Ralph protested. "Far too many folk about then. We need the cover of darkness."

"Fine. Then we'll all meet back tomorrow afternoon here to prepare for—"

"No time!" Ralph persisted. "How long do you think it will take Groby to realize his docking slip is missing and figure out what we'll do? It's dark *now*, my friends!"

The three of them exchanged glances, and without another word needing to be said, they made quickly for the door.

Chapter Thirteen
Tower Wharf

With Ralph taking the lead, the newly-formed team slipped silently through the night-time thoroughfares of London. The more important streets were lit by lanterns, and by law people were supposed to hang candles or lanterns outside their houses at night for the benefit of pedestrians, but few bothered. On some streets, linkboys might sometimes be found carrying flaming torches, and for a small fee they would light the way for travellers. But Ralph stuck to the unlit side streets and alleys as they made their way to the docks, seeming to know every inch of the city's maze of streets like the back of

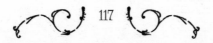

his hand – which Beth suspected he probably did. It was quiet by this time, but every now and then they came across some theatre-goer straggling homeward, a group leaving a tavern, or some other late-night wanderer. Where possible, they crossed the street or darted from one narrow lane into a yet narrower one, always glancing back furtively over their shoulders to make sure they weren't being followed.

When the stink of dead animals and human waste began to sting Beth's nostrils, she knew they were near the river - the place where it was all too easy for Londoners to dispose of anything and everything they no longer needed. John stuck close to her, and although she worried a little about how he would cope if danger struck, the way he had met the challenge when she had beckoned him on stage gave her hope. And anyway, even though Ralph Chandler's underworld skills might prove useful, it was good to have the company of someone "normal", a young man who was not caught up in darker side of life – not to mention someone who seemed good-hearted and who she felt she could trust. She tried to tell herself that the fact that he was good-looking had nothing to do with her professional assessment...

When they found themselves swallowed by the shadows of the daunting walls of the Tower of London, a grey hulking presence against the black sky, Beth knew the wharf was only a short walk away. They all instinctively slowed to a more cautious pace. It was hard to see each other's faces, but Beth somehow sensed that John was growing increasingly edgy.

"How do you fare, John?" she said.

"To be truthful," he whispered, "I'm petrified. But my determination to rescue my friend is greater than my fear."

Beth reached out for his hand and gave it a squeeze of reassurance. She heard him give what sounded like a rather self-conscious swallow and smiled a little to herself in the darkness.

They came to a huge warehouse, one of several that lined the river here, and Ralph led them along its back wall to the corner. They peered warily around towards the wharf and the river. Beyond the shadowy outline of piles of packing cases, barrels, and the wooden cranes like long-necked birds perched on the river bank, they could make out the naked black masts of numerous moored ships swaying gently on the current.

"Lord!" Ralph groaned. "So many ships! T'will take us

all night just to find the right one, let alone search her."

John stepped in front of him, gazing intently into the darkness. "No. No, it won't." Beth tried to follow his direction of sight, which seemed to be fixed on one particular vessel. "I know the ship we want. I shall never forget her outline as long as I live." He broke cover and began to stride towards the river – but Ralph pulled him back by the tail of his coat.

"*Wait!*"

Beth immediately saw why – a night watchman carrying a lighted torch suddenly came into view. He slowly plodded across the wharf, glancing left and right in a weary manner, then disappeared round the front of the warehouse.

"Give him a few moments to get clear," Ralph whispered, "then we must move quickly, for he'll return in fifteen minutes."

Beth frowned at him. "You've done this before!"

"There's rich pickings on them ships if you know where to look."

"You're a thief as well as a pirate?" John hissed, exasperated.

"Someone who makes use of what others has left carelessly lying about, I prefer to call it," Ralph retorted.

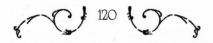

"But I've left that life behind me now. Now stop yer yacking and get ready to move."

He set off at a brisk pace with his peculiar sailor's gait. Beth grabbed John's arm and they quickly followed, heading towards the sound of water lapping against the hulls of the ships. Within a few seconds they were alongside the pitch-black hull of the ship John had pointed out to them.

"You sure this is it?" Ralph queried. "All these boats looks alike to me. I don't know how anyone can be expected to tell the difference."

"I'll prove it to you," John replied confidently. "She's got *Doodgaan* written in red on the side at her prow, remember?"

Beth and Ralph followed him as he crept towards the front of the vessel.

"The name is right here…" Then John's confident tone faded into the darkness of the night, leaving him staring at the blank planking of the ship. "But…?"

"See – they *are* all the same," Ralph grumbled. "Could be *any* of these leaky old tubs. Better start searching, then. No time to waste."

He began to steal towards the ship moored beside the one they had examined. John hesitantly followed,

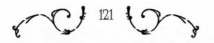

still looking over his shoulder to where he had expected to see the painted name, but Beth lingered behind. She could smell something – something mingled in with the distinctive pitch and tar used to make a ship's planking watertight, and the miles of limp, sea salt-infused rigging. She shuffled right to the edge of the dock and leaned as far out over the river as far as she dared, sniffing like a bloodhound.

"Paint!" she hissed at last, causing John and Ralph to come scurrying back. "Look! From here you can see a patch of planking glistening. It's freshly dried paint – they've tried to hide her name!"

"I *knew* it!" John said a little too loudly.

"*Sssh!*" Ralph whispered, pulling John down into a crouch suddenly. Beth ducked down too, spotting the night watchman on his return journey. They were in the open this time, with nothing to take refuge behind. The shadow cast by the ship made them virtually invisible at least, but if the watchman had heard John's voice or caught sight of them moving around, they were done for...

The light from his lantern kept spreading across the wharf as he steadily swung it left and right, casting his gaze all around. Was the light strong enough to reach

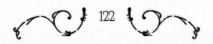

their hiding place? Beth held her breath, watching where the beam fell. He had altered his course slightly to avoid a barrel, and was now heading much closer than she had expected. He extended the lantern to his right again, its pale yellow light picking out the thick mooring cable of the ship two ahead of the *Doodgaan*, making the drops of water hanging from the rope glisten like jewels. They were about to be lit up like actors on a stage!

Ralph had figured this out too. "Run for it!" he hissed.

John started to bob up, but Beth pressed down on his shoulder. "No! Ralph! Stay put. If we move now we'll be seen for sure, and if we're discovered meddling around here they'll probably move the ship. We cannot ruin this chance. We must only run if we know he's seen us."

"I know what Captain Jack Turner of the *Revenge* would do!" John whispered suddenly as the night watchman's light played against the side of the last ship before theirs.

"Oh, splendid," Ralph muttered. "And how do you propose we send for him?"

Beth grinned. "He's right here!"

"Eh?"

Just as the approaching man was about to bring his

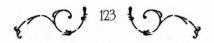

lantern back to the right and bathe them in its light, John scooped up a handful of gravel from the dockside and threw it towards the warehouse. It rattled against the wooden doors and walls, and the night watchman spun quickly round. He held his lantern in that direction and pulled a wooden club from his belt, advancing like a tiger on the prowl.

"Aye-aye, captain!" Ralph whispered, patting John on the back. "All aboard!"

They quickly but stealthily scampered up the gangway and onto the mysterious *Doodgaan*.

"Let's start with the living quarters," Beth suggested. "I'll start with the captain's cabin, you two make your way through the smaller ones."

"Fine," Ralph said quickly.

"All right," John said, his voice shaky.

In almost total darkness, Beth had to feel her way cautiously around the unfamiliar surroundings of the vessel with her hands outstretched like a blind woman, bumping into casks and cannon, entangling herself in ropes. She tried to steady her pounding heartbeat as she slowly led them to a gangway and down some steps leading to the lower deck. Were they alone? Could someone burst out at them at any moment?

Once at the bottom she could just make out a large door ahead of her that could only be the captain's quarters. She eased it open as quietly as she could while the others broke away and commenced their own searches. She could hear the patter of Ralph's distinctive footsteps next door as she navigated her way among the chairs and big table in the centre.

But it was hopeless. Even though there was a large window built into the stern, it was dark outside, and there simply wasn't enough light for her to be able to make out anything at all, other than the shadowy outlines of the cabin furniture, and a candle in the middle of the table that she couldn't possibly light without giving them all away. But as she felt her way around she came across what had to be the captain's cot – an open, coffin-like wooden box, which hung from the beams above so that when the ship rolled it swung freely and didn't tip its occupant out.

Beth grabbed the top sheet from the bed and held it up against the stern window. Easily big enough! She stuffed the corners into the slight gaps between the window and the frame and wherever else she could feel a little nook or cranny with her fingers. Within seconds she had completely covered the window. Next she shuffled to the

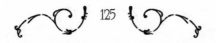

table and felt for the candle and the tinderbox that was beside it. In no time at all, the cabin was illuminated – dimly but quite adequately – in the soft flickering yellow light, and finally Beth could begin to explore properly.

But she had barely commenced when she heard the door creak open; she swivelled sharply about to see two eyes appear round the gap.

"Oh, *very* cosy!" Ralph chimed. "Can't see a thing in the other cabins, but I'm a bit of an expert at searching dark rooms for … let's say 'lost property' and the like, and from what I can tell they're empty – just seems to be the odd chair, bed and so on. I reckon they've started stripping her bare already. Any luck in here?"

"I was just going to look inside this sea chest," she said, starting again for a moment as John came into the quarters, looking pale.

"Anything?" Beth asked him, but he shook his head.

"I kept thinking I heard someone, though…" he said shakily.

Ralph rolled his eyes, and they turned back to the large wooden trunk under the stern window. To her irritation, Beth discovered it was locked.

"How about using this?" John said, his colour beginning to recover. Whoever had been the captain

had left a sword hanging from a nail, and he grabbed it. "Looks stout enough. See if you can prise it open."

When she first inserted the tip of the blade into the thin space under the lid and heaved, the end snapped off. But there was just enough of a gap to jam the thicker, jagged end back in. Within thirty seconds and a lot of yanking, she had levered the lid off and was rummaging inside. "Just bedding, clothes, navigation instruments … Oh, hang on…"

Her fingers had come into contact with something hard hidden inside a folded-up blanket. Unwrapping it, she pulled out a small, slim wooden box with an ornately carved lid. She lifted it carefully and saw just one item inside: a folded letter bearing a red seal.

"Open it!" Ralph urged her.

Beth turned to him with a raised eyebrow. "My, it's a good thing you're here, Ralph. That would never have occurred to me!"

"Some people will tell you sarcasm's the lowest form of wit…"

Ignoring him, Beth broke the seal, carefully unfolded the single page and read:

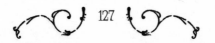

311064

YJJ GQ QCR
UC DMJJMU AYRCQZWQ JCYB
UFCL RFC QUGLC ZSPLQ
RFC PCNSZJGA QFYJJ PGQC YEYGL

John peered over her shoulder. "It's just nonsense…"

"Looks like the sort of thing I'd write – and I *can't* write!" Ralph added, looking over her other shoulder.

But Beth had come across this sort of thing before during her instruction with Alan Strange. "It's a cipher."

"A what?" Ralph queried.

Beth sighed. "Don't you remember your training? A cipher – a message written using some sort of code. To work out what it means we either need to find they key to the code, or work it out for ourselves."

"Well, I can already tell you who *sent* it," John announced. He had been examining the red wax seal under the light from the candle. "This is Sir Henry Vale's seal. I have seen this many times on his old correspondence with the Navy Board. And look at the last two letters at the bottom of the letter, separate from the rest. I don't think that's in cipher – I think it's the initials of the writer: HV!"

Then Beth noticed something else. "Look, in the top corner – it could be a date: thirty-one, ten, sixty-four."

"31 October 1664!" John exclaimed.

"But that's only four days ago," said Beth, frowning. "Sir Henry Vale was one of the men behind King Charles I's execution, after the Parliamentary army defeated the Royalists. He was beheaded for high treason two *years* ago…"

"Look," Ralph interrupted. "You can puzzle over your fancy writing at your leisure now we've got the letter. We came here to find out what happened to your friend Will – remember?"

Beth quickly refolded the letter. "He's right. We may not have much time. The only place we have yet to search is down in the hold. Come on!"

They quickly left the captain's cabin and eventually found the hatchway that led down to the bowels of the ship. John held the candle, shielding it as best he could from any draughts while Beth gingerly lowered herself down the steep wooden ladder into the blackness. Even before reaching the bottom rung, the smells assailed her

senses: the ever-present odour of tar, the rancid meat and cheeses of the crew's provisions, the stale urine of rats. She was below the waterline now, a place where daylight never penetrated. John reached down and passed the candle to her, then began to descend himself.

"It doesn't need three of us going," Ralph said. "It's probably best if I keep watch up here."

Beth nodded up at him, then turned back into the darkness. The hold extended for most of the length and width of the ship, with just a few wooden bulkheads to divide up the space. The feeble candlelight could only illuminate a small area around them. As she crept along, shadows from the casks, crates and assorted nautical gear loomed up, danced about them, and then retreated like spectres fleeing from their approach. With every step, she heard the scurrying of rats fleeing into dark corners.

Suddenly, John froze. "What was that?"

"I didn't hear anything…"

"Someone else is in here." He was pointing towards the stern. "We must leave – quickly!"

He began to back up carefully the way they'd come, and Beth turned to follow – but then she heard the sound too. It was a muffled voice, seeming to be calling for help.

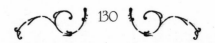

"Wait. It's not a trap – it's someone in need of aid!"

They made their way through the darkness quickly now – and there they saw him, with a gag in his mouth and a great length of chain binding him to the mizzen mast which descended through the ship from the upper deck.

John rushed past Beth and threw himself to his knees beside the figure. "Will! I thought they had killed you!"

Beth gently removed the gag from the young man's mouth. "Two men ambushed me when I came on board…" he gasped, like someone coming up for air after nearly drowning. "Th-they threatened to kill me … Thank God you came!"

"Who were they? Did they sound like Dutchmen?" Beth asked.

Will shook his head. "English. Their leader was an evil man. Talked like he had a sore throat – and as he was tying me I noticed he had a finger missing from one hand." Beth and John exchanged glances. "You know who it is?"

"His name is Edmund Groby," said John.

"What we don't know," said Beth, "is what exactly he's up to."

"All I know is that there was something down here he

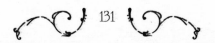

131

didn't want me to see."

John tugged at the chains and examined the lock that kept them taut round his friend's middle.

Will gave a humourless laugh. "No use, John. They're strong and tight – I can barely breathe."

"We must find out what Groby's secret is," Beth said urgently, casting her eyes around the hold.

"What about Will?" John said. "We can't just leave him like this."

"While we're searching, we can look out for any kind of tool lying about that we can use to break the lock."

Beth began to search to one side of Will, and John the other. There were casks of rum, spare sails and spars, but nothing that looked remotely like the sort of thing that Edmund Groby would go to such lengths to keep secret.

"Beth – shine your light this way," John called.

She turned and held the candle at arm's length in his direction. He was standing by a big crate, and the label *VIRGINIA TOBACCO* flickered into view. Virginia was the British colony in America where convicts were sent. Why would a ship from Holland, found adrift in England, be carrying American cargo?

"It's odd. I can't smell any tobacco, and it's normally really strong…" John mused, trying to prise the lid open.

"Pass me the candle."

Beth handed it to him. "Let me try," she said, working her smaller fingers into the small crack in the lid.

"Nothing makes sense today," John muttered as she gave it a tug. The wood of the crate creaked and splintered and began to give way. "But at least we might be able to get to the bottom of this…"

They peered inside. "Dust!" she said. "Nothing but a crate of dust!"

"I'm sure I recognize that smell…" John said, almost to himself.

Beth began sifting some of the fine black powder through her fingers, holding it up to the candlelight. "Maybe there's something buried within it. They wouldn't just fill a crate with useless dust, surely?"

She scooped up another handful, and pulled John's hand that held the candle lower towards the hole she'd made, peering closer so that her head was virtually inside the crate. At the same moment, she heard John let out a shrill cry of alarm, snatching the candle back and sending them both tumbling to the deck as he did so.

"Hey!" she complained, rolling onto her back.

"That's not dust," John cried. "It's *gunpowder*!"

Chapter Fourteen

Flight from the *Doodgaan*

John sprang to his feet like a scalded cat, brushing his hands and clothes frantically to rid himself of the deadly substance. Beth set the still-burning candle down on top of a barrel well away from the crate.

"What were they planning to do with *that*?" Will said, still chained to the mast.

"I don't know," Beth replied. "But now we know what Edmund Groby is capable of—"

She was interrupted by an urgent whisper from above. "Someone's coming!" It was Ralph, who had been keeping guard at the hatchway to the deck above.

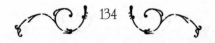

"Up the ladder, quickly!" Beth cried to John.

But Ralph was already sliding down it to join them in the hold. "Too late – they're on deck. Time to play hide-and-seek!" He vanished into the shadows towards the prow of the ship.

"Except the losers don't get another turn…" Beth heard John mutter as he dived – *Captain Jack-style*, she thought – behind a large water cask. Beth hastily replaced the lid of the gunpowder crate, apologized to Will as she shoved the gag back into his mouth, then extinguished the candle and squatted down behind a pile of musty tarpaulin.

Within seconds, she heard the footsteps overhead getting ever closer, and then, just visible in the pitch darkness, she could make the vague outlines of two men clambering down the ladder. One of them was grunting with the effort, and a chill of recognition crept up Beth's spine on hearing the harsh, rasping sound.

Edmund Groby.

"Are you sure about this, master?" came a voice she didn't know.

"Of course," Groby snapped. "People are already asking too many questions. Once the ship is no more, people will wonder about her for a few days and then

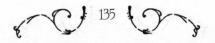

quickly forget. Do it, man."

Beth frowned. *Once the ship is no more?* That didn't sound good…

A flame flared into life, accompanied by a crackling, fizzing sound. Groby and his accomplice clattered back up the ladder quickly.

"*They're going to blow up the ship!*" Beth hissed to her friends as loudly as she dared. "*We need to get out of here!*"

They burst from their hiding place, and Beth gasped as she saw that Groby had lit a long trail of gunpowder heading towards the barrels, like a fuse. She and John desperately tried to scuff out the trail to prevent its progress, but the wooden floorboards had caught alight, and fire was beginning to run rampant in the hold.

"We can't leave Will," John said urgently. "We must try again to free him."

Beth and John hurried over to him. "Try to pull the chain up and over his body," she suggested quickly. They tugged with all their might, but he was shackled so tightly round his chest and beneath his armpits that it was impossible, and he cried out in agony at their futile efforts.

"*Stop, stop!*" he begged.

John grimly wiped the sweat from his brow. "My

friend, even if we have to break your arms or dislocate your shoulders, it will be better than death!"

"That is not what I mean," Will replied, coughing against the smoke beginning to fill the hold from the flames. The orange light from the hissing fuse played across his ghastly pale face, and his terror-filled eyes seemed to be transfixed by it. "Even if you could do it – which I doubt – it would take too long. You must go now. Save yourselves!"

Just then, Beth saw a grubby face appear through smoke. Ralph used one finger to hook the lock holding Will's chains in place, then drop it.

"It's a Robinson number twenty-seven." He sniffed dismissively. "You'd think they'd fork out for something better than that if it's such an important job." He calmly fished a little piece of wire from his pocket.

Beth looked anxiously towards the other side of the hold, where the flames were beginning to lick larger. "Hurry!" she said urgently.

But after a few deft flicks and twists, there was a metallic *click*, and Will wriggled free of his shackles. But instead of heading for the ladder, he tottered on stiff legs towards the crate of gunpowder and the ever-shortening fuse.

"What are you doing?" she cried.

"Go!" he ordered them. "I might not be able to do this."

Beth couldn't believe her ears. "Do *what*?"

"Extinguish the flames. I'm not going to let them destroy the evidence after what they've done to me!"

"I'm off," Ralph muttered, already poised at the bottom of the ladder. "He'll never do it. The fire's already too fierce, the ship will blow any moment—"

"It's impossible Will, you must come now!" John begged his friend. "We can find other evidence…"

Will edged closer. "I shall do this," he called. "Go now! There's no point risking more than one life."

Beth's own mind was in turmoil, but the gunpowder fuse was rapidly burning through and the flames growing more and more intense. She grabbed John by the elbow, ushering him after Ralph. "There's no time to argue. Come on!"

They scrabbled out onto the deck, still gasping from the smoking atmosphere that had begun to envelop the hold. The air outside was cold and fresh, and as she and John scurried across the planking, Beth saw Ralph crouching down in the shadows on the deck, waiting for them on the opposite side of the ship from the wharf.

"Stay down! We can't go that way," he whispered quickly when they reached him. "I think Groby spotted me. I only just managed to hide. He and his bully boy headed off over there thinking they were giving chase…"

Beth and John spun round and saw the two men in the light from the lantern of the night watchman, who had now appeared on the scene. They were covering the only exit to the dockside, looking around in the shadows and frowning.

"You … you mean we should go in the water? I can't swim!" John protested.

"You won't need to." Ralph was tugging on a length of rope that hung over the side of the ship. "There's a boat on the other end of this!"

"Let's go," Beth whispered. "We have to hurry before they spot us."

Beth waited while John cautiously climbed in, then scrambled after him and down into the little rowing boat, from where she reached up and helped Ralph to haul himself in. John grabbed the oars, and soon they were pulling away with the aid of a strongly flowing current.

"I think we've done it." he whispered.

But as they cleared the *Doodgaan* and looked across

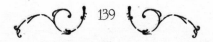

the Thames towards Tower Wharf, they saw Groby shout and point towards them.

"They've spotted us!" Ralph said.

Beth's heart began to pound as she saw the night watchman saying something and pointing along the riverside, then Groby and his henchman began running in that direction. And as John rowed further, they saw what the watchman had been directing Groby towards another boat.

Moments later, Groby and his accomplice had jumped into it and were quickly leaving the dockside. The big man at the oars was straining his broad back, pulling powerfully towards them…

Chapter Fifteen

Shooting the Bridge

"PULL!" shouted Ralph. He struggled to make himself heard over the roar of the water. Now that they were out in the middle of the river, Beth was surprised at how fast and furious the Thames was rushing. She knew that at certain times of the year there were particularly high and strong tides that boosted the river's flow – and this was surely one of those times.

"I *am* pulling!" John gasped, heaving at the oars with all his might.

"Well, they're gaining on us. Let me take an oar and help..." Ralph cried, beginning to rise, but Beth yelled

at him to sit down.

"The interruption will slow us down, or you might upset the boat!"

The only consolation was that their boat was picking up speed because they were going with the surging tidal flow – but so was Groby's boat, and his man was strong enough to row faster than poor John. They were gaining by the second. Beth could now hear Groby's guttural cries as he urged his henchman on, directing threats and curses at them, but his actual words were blurred into one nasty, incomprehensible screech by the noise of the river.

"Pull for the opposite bank, John," Beth urged.

John rested one oar and pulled on the other as he tried to alter course – but as soon as he did so, they were spun sideways so violently by the current that the boat rolled alarmingly and Beth and Ralph had to grab the sides to avoid being thrown out. Freezing cold water sloshed and sprayed into the boat, soaking the three of them. The current was trying to snatch the single oar from John's grasp, and although he managed to get the craft pointing up river again, it was clearly impossible for him to row against the tide to the south bank. And then Beth spotted a new problem ahead.

London Bridge.

She knew that when the river was in this sort of state even experienced watermen hesitated to pass through. For those that braved it, their wary travellers often disembarked, walked past the Bridge, and got back into the boat on the other side. Many times she had passed among the graves of St Katherine's by the Tower and gazed upon stones inscribed *Drowned at the Bridge*…

John had spotted the danger too, and his eyes widened. "What are we going to do?"

"We'll not get through the bloomin" arches alive with the river like *this*!" Ralph yelled.

Groby's vessel was just a boat's length away by now, and Groby himself had moved to the front of his boat. He was holding a long boathook with a vicious-looking curved piece of metal on the end, leaning forward and wielding it like a knight about to go into battle.

"We must take our chances!" Beth shouted. "London Bridge *might* kill us, but Edmund Groby *will*. Aim for the middle arch, John – and hold on tight!"

The closer they got to the monumental old structure, with the houses and shops running along its length making it look more like a little stretched-out town than a bridge, the more the water began to churn and swirl.

The nineteen arches that carried the bridge across the Thames stood on enormous piers. The fast-flowing water was forced between these, causing violent, unpredictable eddies and wildly fluctuating water levels.

Beth clung to the side of the boat with white knuckles, bracing her feet against its timbers. Ralph had curled up into a ball in the bottom, with his arm wrapped round the wooden bench that spanned the width of the craft. John was still bravely fighting the river with his oars, but it was now like being in a watery hurricane and his efforts were useless.

"Let go of the oars! Brace yourself!" Beth screamed, but as the stone pillars loomed rapidly upon them, the roar of the water was so loud that it drowned out her words. And then the oars were ripped from John's grasp anyway and went spinning and bobbing crazily in the foaming current. The boat suddenly began to spin as if in a whirlpool, while at the same time being abruptly lifted on the water backing up against the piers.

The three passengers were thrown one way then another, and suddenly it was all a raging blur and Beth could hardly make sense of what was happening. She felt the boat smash against one side of the pier as they passed under the arch, and there was the sickening sound of splintering wood. Before she could take it all in they were swept against the other side, and she screamed as her fingers were crushed between the pier and the boat. Just as she fell backwards into the bottom, the vessel dropped suddenly, as if it had been swept over a cliff. It must have been a fall of at least six feet, forcing the wind from her lungs on impact. Beth heard an ugly gurgling, gasping noise like a pair of broken bellows, and it took her several seconds to realize that she was making it herself as her own lungs fought to draw air in. Her back felt as if it had been hit with a sledgehammer, and her injured knuckles were on fire. A warm flow of blood trickled down her arms from her hand, but she could make no effort to stop it. She lay stunned, her vision blurred, waiting for the cold waters to take her as the damaged little boat was thrown this way and that. At least then it would be over…

And then everything slowed and quietened.

She blinked away the filthy river water from her eyes and saw twinkling stars floating along serenely above as she lay face upwards. They seemed so strangely peaceful and beautiful that she wondered if she was finally in heaven.

But if so, Ralph was with her. Her daydream-like state

was broken by his spluttering and coughing up water, followed by a string of swear words, some of which even she had never heard before. She eased her aching body into a sitting position and brushed away the sodden russet hair that was plastered across her face. As soon as she was upright, her head began to spin and ache, but the sensation quickly eased. Ralph was lying in a crumpled heap near the stern. Beth could see now that the boat wasn't quite sinking, but was lying low in the water at Ralph's end. Most of the upper stern planking was missing.

Worse still, so was John.

"Look," said Ralph, leaning over the side of their stricken vessel as it drifted on the current, idly turning slow circles as it went.

Beth saw pieces of jagged timber bobbing in the moonlit water all around them – far too much to have come from their damaged stern – and they were being overtaken by an oar that she knew wasn't from their boat.

"Groby's gone to a watery grave if there's any justice!" Ralph muttered darkly.

Beth was already soaked and shivering, but the mention of a "watery grave" sent an extra tremor through her body. "John's out there somewhere too…" she said shakily.

"Sorry, Beth, but even if he survived shooting the bridge, he won't last long when the water's this cold."

She fought back the tears welling up inside her and moved to the opposite side of the boat. "No. No, we're not giving up on him yet," she said determinedly. "Keep looking. You take that side, I'll take this."

They strained their eyes and ears, but the further they drifted without any sign of him, the more their spirits sagged. The rapid current carried them towards the bend in the river near Whitehall Palace, but instead of following the curve their momentum propelled the boat straight on, where it jolted heavily against the wooden posts supporting a jetty outside Worcester House. Beth was sent tumbling into Ralph, and there was an ominous splintering sound from their boat. More of the stern had come away, and a large jagged crack flashed like black lightning across the middle of the stricken craft. Water immediately bubbled up through it and began to fill the boat, and Beth scrambled to her feet, readied herself, then leaped out onto the jetty's stairs. As the boat quickly filled with water swirling around Ralph's legs, she reached across to help him out of the boat too.

They sat shivering and exhausted on the bottom

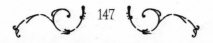

stair, looking on mournfully as their boat finally split in two and both parts quickly slipped beneath the murky surface of the river. Beth knew this area well. Drury Lane was just a short walk from here and it almost felt as if she had come home – but as a failure, and now without John. Neither of them seemed able to move just yet, despite the cold.

"That's it, then…" Ralph sighed. His knees were drawn up with his chin resting on them, his eyes still fixed on the spot where their boat had sunk.

"I – I liked him…" Beth murmured. Blood still trickled from her aching hand, and her back was stiff and sore.

"I could tell…!" Ralph tried to turn it into a light-hearted quip, but there was no conviction in his voice. "Well … at least he managed to save his friend. Will's safe."

"What do you mean?"

"There was no explosion. That amount of gunpowder? We'd have heard it go off if we'd been in a thunderstorm in America!"

Beth realized he was right. "And Groby's gone – so yes, Will must be free. I wonder if he found—"

"What is *that*?" Ralph had risen to his feet and

he was looking out across the Thames back towards London Bridge.

Beth rose also. All she could see was a dark shape floating their way with what looked like a branch with some twigs sticking out of it.

"'Tis a log, that's all."

"I've got eyes like a hawk, me," Ralph said. "It is a log – but that's not all."

As it drew closer, they began to hear something echoing across the water.

Spluttering and coughing.

And then the dark shape sailed into a patch of bright moonlight.

"T'IS JOHN!" Beth exclaimed.

"But the river's going to take him past us," Ralph said quickly. "And he doesn't look in great shape—"

Beth had already seen that, and was moving to the edge of the stairs, crouching.

"Beth, *pleeease* tell me you're not going to do what I think you're going to do…"

"I'm not losing him again," she said through gritted teeth.

"The current's too strong! You'll *both* drown! He might be able to grab…"

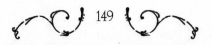

149

But Beth was already launching herself into the air. The icy water took her breath away and paralysed her for a second as she came up gasping from her headfirst dive, but she made herself press on towards the spot where she hoped she could intercept John as he floated towards her. The current fought against her every inch of the way, trying to force her sideways upstream. She struggled against the water, but everything she had been through was quickly catching up with her and her strength was ebbing away by the second. The injured hand and bruised back that Beth had pushed out of her mind now forced themselves into her consciousness with a vengeance; the water was choppy and kept slapping into her face so that she was swallowing and choking on it with almost every stroke.

But still she kept on, and soon John was heading straight for her. She had to stop and tread water for a moment so that she didn't overshoot and miss him. It wasn't until the log he was clinging to was almost upon her that she appreciated just how fast he was being carried along. She reached out and just managed to grab John's coat, but the protruding branch caught her a glancing blow on the cheek and forehead, its twigs missing her eye by a fraction.

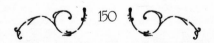

But she had him!

She screamed at John to let go of the log, but although he was conscious, it was as if he was in a trance. He said nothing, just spluttered and gasped and clung grimly to the log. It was his lifeline. She tried to prise his fingers free, but had to keep her own hold at the same time, and it was if his hands were frozen to the wood. In desperation, she manoeuvred her way round him hand-over-hand, using John's clothing to hold onto until she was on the opposite side of the log. Then she began to kick towards Ralph for all she was worth. At first it didn't seem to make any difference, but as they approached the bend in the river where their friend waited, Beth's efforts were rewarded and the log began to cut across the current towards the bank. She wasn't strong enough to steer it to the stairs where Ralph was, but he realized this himself and scurried down to the next landing place. He leaned out and grabbed the helpless John by the collar before the log could speed past, and in the same instant Beth made a leap and managed to catch a rough, splintery wooden post, hauling herself out of the water with her last remaining energy.

Ralph tended to John while Beth flopped onto her back, her chest heaving, her hands so stiff and cold they

151

no longer felt as if they even belonged to her. She felt her mind begin to go blank and soon she had drifted off into unconsciousness...

Chapter Sixteen
The Cipher

By the time Beth came to her senses again and levered herself up onto her elbows, she discovered that both she and John were covered in blankets to keep them warm, though they were still at the bankside. Ralph must have been waiting for their exhaustion to wear off a little before they got moving again, but sleep must have got the better of him too. He was sitting with his back against one of the steps, his head lolling forward, snoring quietly. The blankets were ragged and flea-ridden, and she dreaded to think where he had found them – but they were warm, and she felt a pang of guilt at ever having doubted his honesty.

But soon she recalled that there were more urgent matters than her own feelings to worry about. Memories of what had happened on the *Doodgaan* came flooding back, and she felt inside her cloak, relieved to find that the little wooden box containing the coded letter was still nestling there. She lay back again and fumbled to open out the letter with numb fingers. Dawn was just beginning to break now, and there was just enough light to make out the mysterious jumble of letters on the damp but still preserved paper. She stared at it for a moment, deciding to force her weary, fogged brain to concentrate and recall what Alan Strange had taught her about ciphers. Time could be of the essence…

YJJ GQ QCR

UC DMJJMU AYRCQZWQ JCYB

UFCL RFC QUGLC ZSPLQ

RFC PCNSZJGA QFYJJ PGQC YEYGL

Codecracking was hard enough when she was fresh and able to use a pen and paper. If this was a complex cipher devised by an expert – as it probably was – it would be all but impossible to solve under these circumstances. Still,

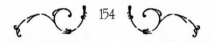

Beth stared at the letters, trying to mentally rearrange them in her head, trying to see a pattern, force them into some sort of order. Lying on her back with the letter held up at arm's length with just the odd white gull flapping across a dirty grey sky to distract her, she blinked, screwed her eyes up and worked her way through the message again and again.

John began to stir beside her. First there was a grunt, then he suddenly sat bolt upright with a panicked cry. He threw his blanket off and began to rise, looking about him as if ready to escape from some imaginary enemy.

Beth laid an arm on his shoulder. "Be still, John. You're safe among friends."

He managed to focus on her, then glanced across at Ralph. "Lord … I dreamed that Edmund Groby had me in shackles, and he was just about to—"

"Groby is no more," Ralph croaked, rousing himself into full wakefulness and stretching his arms out wide to get rid of the stiffness.

"We *think* he is no more," Beth corrected him. "But we do know his boat was dashed to pieces…"

Now John noticed the letter in Beth's hand. "Oh – thank goodness you managed to hang onto it. Have you been able to work out what it means?"

She shook her head. "I need time and writing implements…"

"Probably doesn't matter," Ralph offered. "I dare say it just says 'Kill John Turner and his accomplices.'"

"No," said Beth. "Henry Vale would never have heard of John when he wrote this – four days ago. A letter found in a mystery ship loaded with gunpowder has to be of far greater import."

"Gunpowder!" John cried, springing up again. "Will!"

"Will's probably a lot warmer and comfier than us, my friend," Ralph reassured him.

"The ship didn't blow up – we'd have heard it," Beth explained.

John exhaled with relief. He took the letter from Beth and scrutinised it. "There *is* some sort of logic to it … Will and I used to send each other coded messages at work making fun of our senior officers when we were bored. Look at how 'RFC' crops up twice. 'The' is one of the most common words, so the letters representing it would likely crop up several times. In *our* notes, we would simply use the next letter to the one that was intended – so A would be B, B would be C and so on, so perhaps—"

"No, I've tried that and it still makes no sense," Beth

told him quickly. "Besides, people such as the ones we are dealing with would never use such a childish cipher."

"I was only trying to help…"

"Oh, I didn't mean *you* are childish, John. Just that such a code could be so easily broken that a spy would never dare use it."

"Unless he was in a hurry…" Ralph chipped in.

"What do you mean?" asked Beth.

"Sir Henry Vale was supposed to have snuffed it. Somebody, somehow, saved his neck — but it must all have been done in haste. What if there was no time to work out a really tough code? What if it the person it's intended for didn't know the key, so Vale *had* to risk making it a code that anyone could work out? At least," Ralph added sheepishly, "someone who knows their letters, not like me…"

"Something more simple…" Beth pondered, then suddenly snatched the letter back from John. She involuntarily flushed with embarrassment as she studied it. "You're right, John. I should not have been so hasty to doubt you. It's a classic, simple three-letter shuffle!"

"Sounds like a dance!" he said.

"The three-letter shuffle simply means you have two alphabets side by side, and just move one forward or

back three places so that A becomes Y or C, B becomes Z or D and so on. It just seemed so unlikely that someone might use it…" she said sheepishly.

"That's what you get for trying to show off, eh?" Ralph said, but his teasing grin made Beth relent from the retort that was on the tip of her tongue. "So what happens to the letters that go off the bottom?"

"They go to the start. Y becomes A, and Z becomes B if moving on." She looked at the message again. "But if R becomes T, then the letters here were moved *back* to code the message, so we have to move them *on* to decode it."

They all gathered around in a circle, sitting cross-legged. With growing excitement Beth called out the letters while John worked out what real letter they represented. Each time they got one he etched the word in the muddy ground using a stick. Finally, a message of sorts appeared before their eyes: ragged and faint in places, but clear enough.

ALL IS SET

FOLLOW CATESBY'S LEAD

WHEN THE SWINE BURNS

THE REPUBLIC SHALL RISE AGAIN

"Hmm…" said John, deflated.

The air of expectancy was quickly dampened by the dirt-scrawled message. It was in recognizable English, yet still appeared to make little sense. They stared at the ground, perplexed.

"Clear as mud, then!" Ralph commented laconically after a while.

"It's not funny!" Beth snapped, but found herself having to stifle a giggle – and she saw John doing the same. Before she knew it they were all laughing so hard that tears came to their eyes. Beth was vaguely aware that the remark wasn't *that* funny – but after all they had been through, she thought they were all feeling almost hysterical.

"If only we knew who Catesby is," said Ralph, once they had calmed down.

"Yes," agreed Beth. "The name sounds familiar, but—"

"Oh, I know who Catesby was," said John. "Everyone thinks that Guy Fawkes was at the head of the Gunpowder Plot, but he was just the man who was given the job of lighting the fuse. Robert Catesby was the leader – the brains behind the whole plan."

"Of course!" Beth cried. "So what have we got? 'Follow Catesby's lead…'"

"That's obvious, even if you don't know your letters." Ralph snorted. "Gunpowder under the Houses of Parliament! The Republicans hate our King, so he must be the 'swine'…"

"So, we follow Catesby's lead, which takes us into Parliament with another Gunpowder Plot?" said Beth, her eyes widening. "Can they really mean to try it again?"

John bit his lip thoughtfully. "Parliament is searched from top to bottom every Fifth of November these days and Vale would know that, no matter how hurriedly this was planned."

An image of Big Moll flashed into Beth's mind, and for a minute should couldn't work out why. But then it came to her. "The King isn't going to Parliament on the fifth anyway! He's attending the bonfire feast at the Tower to commemorate the discovery of the Plot."

"*That's* where they'll be lying in wait for him!" exclaimed John.

"No doubt using gunpowder removed from the *Doodgaan*!" Ralph added. "The barrel we found was just the leftovers – the rest will likely be hidden in the bonfire. Unless someone can stop it, the King will be blown up on the morrow!"

"No," said Beth, gazing at the dark spire of St Martin-

in-the Fields, silhouetted against the hazy daylight spreading across the eastern horizon. "We have just a few hours to act – it already *is* the morrow!"

Chapter Seventeen
Refuge

Beth didn't know quite what time it was as she, John and Ralph made their way towards the Peacock and Pie in the soft early morning half-light, but few people were up and about yet. There was just the odd market trader and waterman making their way to work, and every now and then a stray dog skulking in an alleyway barked at them as they passed. Still, she was glad to be making her way home so she could recuperate fully and decide what they ought to do next after their startling discovery. When they arrived at Covent Garden, they came to a halt.

"We must go find Alan Strange and tell him about

162

the plot to kill the King," Ralph said.

Beth nodded. "Perhaps you ought to go. John and I may need to recover our strength a little more. We shall wait at the tavern 'til we hear what he wants us to do."

"Very well. I'll signal old Strange with the cathedral bell's toll. When you hear the signal, you'll know his instructions shouldn't be far behind."

Just after he had turned away and begun to head off, Beth called after him. "Ralph…"

"Yes?"

"Thanks for the blankets … And I'm sorry I didn't trust you earlier."

He flashed her a dirty-toothed grin. "If you'd trusted me before you knew more about me, I wouldn't have trusted *you* – because I'd have known you were a rotten spy!"

Beth sat before the wide, deep fireplace of the Peacock and Pie, glad to be finally warming herself after their freezing, watery exploits of the previous night. She had changed into clean clothes and was already feeling like she could think more clearly, ready to take on whatever they

163

had to face next to stop the plot to kill King Charles...

Big Moll, whom they'd found already up and bustling about in preparation for the big day when they arrived, had let John go up and change into some spare clothes belonging to one of the potboys who worked in the tavern. As soon as Beth spotted him when he came back downstairs, she had to quickly turn away and suppress a giggle. The potboy was barely half John's size, and the sleeves of the blue doublet ended well short of his wrists. The grey breeches were similarly skimpy, and the dirty white stockings came only halfway up his calves, exposing a pair of very white and rather knobbly knees.

"Something ails you, Beth?" he said through clenched teeth and a reddening face.

She wiped her eyes, gave a little cough, and turned to face him. "Just a frog in my throat..."

His eyes narrowed. "I have learned a lot about spying in a short time, and I believe I can tell when someone is telling the truth or having sport with me."

She didn't have the heart to tell him the truth, but he cast his eyes over his new attire and sniffed, with a twinkle in his eye, "'Tis the new fashion from France."

They both dropped their pretences and began to laugh, and John joined her at the fire.

"I wonder what task Mister Strange will have us perform to prevent Vale's plot?"

"*Us?*" Beth asked with a crooked smile. "So you are one of his spies now too?"

"I … well … I thought…"

"Well, John Turner, you are *not* one of Alan Strange's secret agents…" She let the pause linger in the air as long as she dared. "But Captain Jack of the *Revenge* will no doubt be vital to the success of our mission!"

John grinned. "I cannot promise *he* will always be on hand, but *I* will always do my best."

Beth reached across spontaneously and squeezed his hand. "You have already more than proved yourself. You really *are* like Captain Jack, you just need to believe it."

He blushed and avoided her eyes – but didn't hurry to let go of her hand. "This all seems like a far cry from my ordinary life," he sighed. "I've become accustomed to just doing my frankly rather mundane work, and then coming home to six brothers and sisters all getting underfoot – well, apart from sweet Polly. Polio has shrivelled her legs, so we have to take extra special care of her. But there are nine of us with my mother and father, all squeezing into our little house in Shadwell, trying to make ends meet … I never thought this sort of adventure was even possible!"

Beth smiled at the mention of John's home life, and something inside her still ached for the warmth of a home with a mother and father, even if it were cramped and difficult…

"What's wrong?" John asked, his eyes narrowing with concern.

"Oh, nothing. But you should count yourself lucky to have your family around you," she replied.

"Did you…?" He hesitated, and then started again. "Did you grow up nearby? With your family, I mean?"

Beth shrugged. "Not too far. I was a foundling, left at Bow Church. But I did have a family, for a time – I was adopted." She swallowed. "It was a happy life, but my adoptive parents died quite close to one another when I was young. I think when Mister Johnson died, his wife was left broken-hearted, literally. And after that…" She trailed off, shaking her head, and John reached out to touch her arm.

"I'm sorry," he said, looking at her with a furrowed brow. "I didn't mean to upset you."

Beth shook her head once more, and swiftly dashed a tear away from the corner of her eye. "It was difficult, that's all. I was taken in by a neighbour who seemed

 166

pleasant at first, but soon I was being treated as the family slave. They were … they were awful. Eventually I had to run away, and that's when I joined the theatre. *They* were like my family during that time, and they still are, in a way. But I think it was all that experience made me so well-suited to this life," she lowered her voice, "as a spy." She forced a smile, and soon found it turn into a genuine grin as John returned it. "I'm tougher than I look," she finished.

"That's for certain," John said, seeming relieved that she was less upset.

"And now we have a real plot on our hands. But whatever Alan Strange has in mind for us," said Beth at last, "I think I have an idea of my own."

"Shouldn't we wait to see what he says? I don't want to get the sack before he even knows I'm working for him!"

Beth laughed. "Whatever his thinking is, we know one thing: *someone* must get into the great bonfire feast at the Tower. *I* know how we can ensure it is us."

"How?"

"Well, you have already stolen the clothes of one of her boy servants – why not steal his job as well? They will be expecting Moll to take at least a couple of helpers with her. Why not us?"

"Even if Groby's dead his people are bound to be there. What if we are recognized?"

"We shall just have to have our wits about us. We have overcome greater challenges."

Moll walked past them carrying a large tray of sweetmeats in her great hands. "You two rogues warmed yer bones up yet? Goodness knows what you were up to…"

"Er, yes thanks, Moll," Beth said quickly. "You look very busy."

"Rushed off me feet, I am! But there's nothing wrong with a bit o' hard work, that's what my old ma used to say."

"Still, I wager you would appreciate a little help…?"

Big Moll raised an eyebrow. "You volunteering, like?"

Beth gave John the faintest of meaningful smiles. "Well, 'the Devil makes work for idle hands' – that's what *you* always say."

Moll threw her head back, guffawing in her unique, booming way. "Why do I always think there's something else going on behind your words, young lady? Not been raining lately as I recall…" she said, eyeing their wet, bedraggled clothes as they hung to dry, and then Beth's scratched face and the cuts to her knuckles. "But if you're truly offering, I won't look a gift horse in the mouth."

"We are happy to help," John chimed in.

"That settles it then, you can both come with me to the Tower!" She leaned forward and peered at them melodramatically. "But mind you behave in there. It's the sort of place you never come out of alive if you cross them!"

"Yes, we know," said Beth, rather more sombrely than she'd intended. "Uh, is Maisie awake?"

"Well, if she isn't, she should be. Why don't you go and find out, Mistress Beth?"

Beth left John sitting by the fire and made her way upstairs to the chamber where she and Maisie lodged. Watery sunlight was seeping in through the window and falling on the sleeping figure, lighting up the soft white skin of Maisie's face and the mass of brown curls round her head scattered over the pillow. Beth hated to wake her. She bent over her friend and very gently touched her arm. Maisie's eyelids flickered, then her blue eyes opened.

"Beth! You didn't come home last night…"

"I … I had a few things to take care of. I just wanted to see how you are – and let you know I'm afraid I'm going to be leaving you again for a while. I'll be helping Big Moll at the King's bonfire feast."

Maisie sat up eagerly. "Can I come?"

Beth winced inwardly. She knew this would happen, but if it all went wrong, she wanted to have said a proper goodbye. Her heart sank at the thought. "It's best if you don't. There are still people who wish King Charles had never come to the throne – that we could go back to being a republic like in Cromwell's time. They … they might just do something at such a big gathering as this."

Maisie grabbed Beth's hand. "There isn't going to be a big fight or something, is there? You're not placing yourself in danger?"

"I dare say nothing will happen. I'm just saying that this is the sort of occasion where it *might*…" Beth forced a smile. "And anyway, who will look after the tavern while Moll's away if you're not here?"

"I suppose so…"

It hurt Beth to see her friend's downcast expression, but she would rather that than expose Maisie to some of the things that had happened lately.

Suddenly she heard a sound that made her look up. Her eyes were drawn to the window and out past the rooftops and smoking chimneys towards St Paul's Cathedral. The bells had begun to toll.

She counted five peals, a pause, then a sixth.

Ralph was sending his message to Alan Strange – their attempt to stop the plot to kill the King had begun.

Chapter Eighteen
The Tower

It wasn't a long way from the Peacock and Pie to the Tower of London – but it certainly felt it, Beth decided, when you had a tray of pies balanced on your head. Big Moll had taught them the method, which was a common-enough sight on the streets of London. However, it was nowhere near as easy as Moll herself made it look as she marched ahead of them, dodging between carriages and people on horseback, and ducking under the low-slung signs hanging outside almost every shop along the way.

The Fifth of November was an eagerly awaited day of celebration, and all of London knew about the glorious

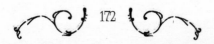

feast at the Tower that would be attended not only by the great and good, but the King himself. Yet at the same time Beth knew that she and John were walking into danger, with only a vague idea of what to expect. Now that Groby was most likely out of the way, she wasn't even too sure who to look out for. They walked along Thames Street past the Custom House, and the soaring grey walls of the impenetrable fortress came into view. Beth knew that the Tower was much more than just that. It was a citadel with inner and outer walls, protecting the Crown Jewels. It was a royal palace and armoury. It was a place of imprisonment, and execution: Moll had told her this was where Guy Fawkes had been tortured here after his arrest. They had to make sure it wasn't also to go down in history as the place where a king was assassinated...

The guards at the Wharf Gate looked fearsome at first sight: tall and erect with their armour and pikestaffs, but it was soon apparent that they knew Big Moll well, and they ushered her straight in without a second glance at her young helpers. They made their way to the kitchens, crossing the inner ward, but as they did, John stopped and pointed at a mountain of logs, planks and other wooden scraps.

"Look over there!"

"Yes. That's where it will happen," Beth whispered as she followed his gaze. "The King is going to light the bonfire to officially open the proceedings. When he does, if those conspirators have their way – BOOM!"

"Unless we can prevent it…"

"We *will* prevent it, Captain Jack!"

When they entered the cavernous kitchens, the sights and sounds took Beth's breath away. The heat and roaring flames from the big open fires and ovens made it seem at first like an entrance to Hell itself, and her senses were assailed by the smells of roasting and baking mingled with the odour of human sweat from the toiling staff. The cooks shouted to their skivvies, and it was all a strange mixture of pandemonium and order, with everyone scurrying about like ants yet seeming to know what they were doing. Over on the far side she saw two cooks working on the biggest hog she had ever seen in her life. One was rubbing oil onto its enormous expanse of skin, while the other sprinkled pepper and herbs along its length.

"Ain't that a beauty!" Moll declared. "First slice will go to the guest of honour – King Charles himself!"

"You could fit the house where I live inside this place and still have plenty of room to spare!" said John, gaping

at this strange new world.

Moll lifted the tray from her head as easily as man might take his hat off, and plonked it down on a long wooden table that was clean but bore the marks of many years of hot trays, sharp knives and cleavers. "Put yours beside mine," she barked at John, seeming to come into her element in this place. "And yours over there beside that oven," she told Beth. "Keep an eye out for 'em. Good food has been known to go missing in this place. The King will want fresh food, so there's more baking to be done – follow me."

Soon they had obtained the ingredients to make more pies and sweetmeats, and Big Moll left them to their tasks of preparing and chopping the herbs and vegetables while she commenced the kneading and rolling out of pastry with her burly arms and hands, humming tunelessly to herself as she worked.

As soon as she dared, Beth sidled closer to John and spoke quietly into his ear. "I'm going to slip outside to take a closer look at that bonfire. If anyone asks, tell them I needed to visit the water closet."

John nodded without looking up or pausing from his labours. Beth slipped away from the table and headed for the exit, but she was stopped short by a booming

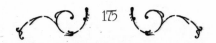

male voice aimed in her and John's direction.

"Hey, you two – go and fetch some mead up from the cellars." It was one of the head chefs.

Beth hesitated. "But … I was just going to—"

"No 'buts' in here!" Moll cried, overhearing the conversation. "Do as the man says. Chop-chop!"

"Er, where is the cellar?" John asked.

"Outside, first door on the left," the man told them. "You'll need the key – here."

Reluctantly, Beth took the big iron key, and she and John left their task and walked swiftly towards the exit. But once they were outside, Beth held John back and slowed their pace down to as leisurely a crawl as she dared without making them look suspicious.

"At least this gives us a chance to take a good look around," she whispered.

John looked over in the direction of the gigantic unlit bonfire. "Beth, look. What are *they* up to?"

There were two men in guards' uniforms lurking on the side of the wood pile furthest away from prying eyes, constantly checking over their shoulders. One stopped and crouched down and seemed to be trying to peer into the centre of the pile.

"I don't know," replied Beth. "But I'd wager they're

up to no good. They might be laying the gunpowder now, even. When the King lights the bonfire, the whole place – him and us included – will be blown sky-high. We have to figure out a way to stop this…"

They had come almost to a halt as they watched the guards, but the man who had been looking into the fire straightened up suddenly and looked in their direction. Beth and John hurried on, but then noticed a distant figure walking towards them.

"That's Sir Roger Fortescue!" John said. "He's the Commissioner of the Navy Board."

"The man you said was present when Arthur Jones had his throat cut?"

"Yes. He was likely invited to the celebrations, but to be here so early? I think he must be right at the centre of this whole plot. But no one would ever believe us if we accused him…"

Beth stopped walking, her eyes widening with excitement. "No – but if we could get him out of the way, it might delay or prevent the plot!"

"How? There's a chance he'll recognize me—" John began.

"Then leave it to me and hide – quick!"

Fortescue was still some distance away, and it looked

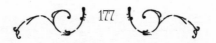

as though he was walking towards the guards by the fire. John veered to his left and ducked behind a large bin of food waste. Thinking quickly, Beth ran to the cellar door and used the key they'd been given to open it, then held out a corner of her dress and shut the door on it so that it was trapped. When Sir Roger Fortescue came a little closer, she called out to him in a pathetic voice.

"Sir! If you please, sir!"

The rotund commissioner turned to face her, his chubby features displaying a flash of anger at being summoned by a lowly servant. But the sight of a beautiful young girl in distress caused the dark cloud to lift immediately, and he waddled towards her.

"Perhaps I can be of some assistance, my dear?"

"My dress seems to be caught. I don't know if it's a nail or splinter … and the door seems to be jammed…!"

He patted her on the cheek with a podgy hand. "Never fear, Fortescue is here!"

He turned the knob and gave the door a good push. It opened easily, and as soon as it did Beth put her boot to his enormous bottom and propelled him forcefully down the steps and into the darkness. She heard his howls of indignation as she swiftly slipped the key in the lock and turned it again.

"Beth!" John hissed, half in horror and half in admiration, emerging from his hiding place.

She simply smiled and brushed her hands together in the way she often saw Moll do. "Let's go. Chop-chop!"

Chapter Nineteen

An Unwelcome Return

Sir Roger Fortescue's curses and cries for help could still be heard as Beth and John walked away from the cellar, but more and more people were arriving for the great feast now – not just staff, but guests too in all their finery were milling around. To Beth's relief, it soon became apparent that there was so much excited talking, shouting and singing that his pleas would be drowned out. There was also a distant crackle of smaller bonfires being lit around the city. It was already late afternoon and growing dusky. The celebration at the Tower was far from the only one; all over London ordinary people were

beginning to light their own fires: in gardens, on waste ground and even street corners. Soon the first fireworks were streaking into the air, and smoke from fires drifted over the Tower's walls.

As they hurried away towards the kitchens, a shabby figure came looming out of the pall of smoke and the gathering crowd, ambling towards them.

"Ralph!" John said. "How did you find us?"

He tapped the side of his nose. "One of me many skills!"

"What news from Alan Strange?" Beth asked quickly.

Ralph's face darkened. "He didn't turn up."

Beth felt a chill like an icy breeze pass right through her. "What? But even I heard the bells – the special signal?"

Ralph shook his head. "I waited, but he didn't turn up. I looked everywhere. The place was deserted – everyone getting ready for the bonfire celebrations."

"Something's not right," Beth said through clenched teeth.

John's eyes widened. "Surely if they've got to your spymaster himself, we are in great danger—"

"Why, look – it's Beth!" a jolly voice interrupted them.

The players and behind-the-scenes folk from the King's Theatre were coming their way, led by the manager William Huntingdon. There was quite a crowd of them, including Beth's arch-enemy Benjamin Lovett, who was wearing his most flamboyant wig and resplendent clothes.

Beth liked Huntingdon, but he could hardly have chosen a worse time to arrive. She did her best to put on a cheerful face. "Mister Huntingdon! I'm glad you could all make it."

"I didn't know you were coming, Beth."

"She's helping our landlady with the pies!" cried a voice from among Huntingdon's group. Beth's heart sank even further. It was an excited Maisie. "Big Moll makes the best pies in all London!"

"Maisie!" Beth said, trying to keep the forced smile on her face as her heart sank. "I thought you were looking after the Peacock and Pie?"

"Oh, Moll's sister came – turned out it had been arranged all along. Then I saw Mister Huntingdon passing the tavern on his way to the Tower, and he invited me to join them!"

"That's wonderful…" Beth said, taking her friend by the arm and leading her away from the rest of the group.

She couldn't reveal just how much danger Maisie was in without making her panic and perhaps even drawing attention to what she, John and Ralph were up to. But there was no guarantee they would succeed in stopping the explosion, and she had to do something to ensure Maisie's safety. "But I really do think you ought to be helping out at the tavern. Moll was expecting it, and we wouldn't want to let her down. There is to be a big bonfire party at the end of Drury Lane, so you won't miss out."

Maisie's crestfallen look almost broke Beth's heart. "Oh, well, if you think I should go…"

Beth nodded, and gave her young friend a squeeze round the shoulders to reassure her. "I do, Maisie. It's going to get much too crowded here. In fact, I wish *I* could get away and join you on Drury Lane too…" She noticed that Maisie was looking elsewhere and didn't seem to be listening. Following her friend's gaze, she saw that the colossal hog was being brought out from the kitchen – it took four men to carry it and fix it to the spit over a blazing fire a few feet away from them.

"Oh, can I at least stay for a piece of that?" Maisie asked, licking her lips. "I've been in such a rush I haven't eaten all day – and that looks delicious!"

 183

As the smells from the hog beginning to roast wafted her way, Beth's mouth began to water too. She looked across at where the huge mound of wood for the bonfire stood. It was deserted and there were no signs that it was going to be lit for some time.

"Well, I suppose it wouldn't do any harm just to—" She froze in mid-sentence.

"Beth?" Maisie said. "What is it?"

"It" was a cook with his back to Beth. A short and stocky cook turning the roasting spit a couple of times, then muttering something to his assistant that caused them both to leave the hog roasting on just one side while they rushed away.

The hand that had been turning the spit was missing its middle finger.

Groby!

Worse still – much worse – Beth suddenly realized their big mistake. "First slice goes to the guest of honour – King Charles himself," Moll had said.

The gunpowder wasn't hidden in the bonfire – it was inside the enormous hog!

Chapter Twenty

To the River

"Beth?" Maisie repeated disconcertedly.

"What? Oh, sorry, Maisie. I'm just a little distracted…"

But before she had a chance to formulate a plan, the sound of trumpets blaring and people cheering and clapping rose up all around them. She turned towards the Tower's main entrance and saw a large and colourful assembly processing into the grounds.

"The King, the King!" cried Maisie, jumping up and down and clapping her hands. She threw her arms round Beth's shoulders and kissed her on the cheek. "Thank you for letting me stay, Mistress Beth!"

The smell of the pig over the flames became intense, gradually changing from a pleasant smell of roasting meat to an acrid one of scorching. Beth's heart began to pound. How much longer before the powder went up?

"Beth!" came John's voice. He and Ralph had forced their way through the ever-increasing mass of excited Londoners in the Tower's grounds to find them. "I just heard someone talking – the main bonfire isn't to be lit 'til it gets properly dark, and that won't be for a while yet. There's plenty of time to think of a plan!"

"No, there isn't," Beth replied.

"What do you mean?" Ralph queried.

"The gunpowder – it's not in the wood pile!"

"But—" John began.

"When the code said the 'swine shall burn', it wasn't referring to the King. It's *that*." She pointed towards the hog, blackening now underneath. Fat oozed and dripped from its body into the fire, making it spit and crackle fiercely.

John clapped his hands to his head. "No!"

"It's big enough, all right," said Ralph, frowning. "And it looks to me like it's going to blow any second…"

The King's party was ever getting closer, moving slowly through the crowds. Beth began to run towards the spit roast. "Grab one end of the spit!" she shouted to John. "Ralph – we need a distraction!"

"Good as done," he replied quickly.

Beth and John raced over to the hog and grabbed the wooden handles at each end of the spit. It was so heavy they could barely keep it off the ground, but they pulled it away from the roaring fire. By now, though, the animal's body was red-hot and the flesh was even on fire in a couple of places.

"It'll still be cooking on the inside," Beth said urgently to John. "Come on – we have to get it to the river!"

As they struggled with their burden, Beth saw that Ralph was writhing on the stones, clutching his throat and making the most unearthly gurgling noises. An anxious crowd had begun to gather around him, and some of the King's guards even came over to see what was happening.

"Well done, Ralph," Beth muttered to herself. People gave her and John odd looks as they struggled away with the roasting hog, but no one tried to stop them. Soon the river was in sight, and Beth's hopes raised – but the beast was so heavy that their pace was slowing with every step. Beth's shoulder muscles were aching, and at times the hog dragged along the ground and she had to adjust

her grip to keep it up. The animal was still smoking hot and dripping with fat. She could feel the heat from it burning her cheeks and causing beads of sweat to break out on her brow.

"The inside must be like an oven," John yelled breathlessly. "I-I don't think we're going to make it!"

"We must! Come on, John. We've just twenty yards to go!"

But then a cry came from one of the guards. "It's a trick – look over there!"

Beth didn't even need to look back to know they'd been discovered. She heard heavy footsteps thundering in their direction. Only the strongest, fittest and most able soldiers made it into the King's personal guard, and she knew they'd be upon them in moments. She could see the Thames sparkling through Traitor's Gate, which had been left open to allow guests arriving by river to enter – but the stampede of feet was getting louder by the second…

John almost tripped on the cobbles under the arch of Traitor's Gate and the pig scraped along the ground, but he just managed to keep his balance. Beth could now hear an ominous fizzing sound coming from inside the hog's body that reminded her of the fuse on the barrel of gunpowder on the *Doodgaan*, and smoke started to escape from the cooking beast's mouth and nose.

"It's too late! Let's leave it and take cover!" John screamed.

"No! Three more steps and throw!"

"Got you, wench!" came a man's voice close behind her, and Beth felt a heavy hand grabbing the back of her dress and she struggled to tear herself free.

"NOW!" she shouted.

With the man's hand still gripping her dress, she heaved the hog with all her might, and John did the same. As it tumbled over the edge of the river bank, Beth and John dived to the ground, and the guard who had caught them instinctively did the same. The instant the smoking, sizzling animal hit the water there was a tremendous *boom* that shook the stones beneath Beth that felt like a clap of thunder inside her head. Water, stones and soil burst upwards and then rained down from the sky, splattering against her prone body. The waters of the Thames bubbled and fizzed as the debris continued to fall.

Beth raised her head and tried to focus; her vision was blurred but she felt sure that further downstream she saw Groby and his accomplice getting into a boat and

 189

rowing away. She heard voices calling, but her ears were ringing so loudly and painfully that she could make no sense of them. Then, before she could do anything else, she saw the booted feet of two guards running over to her, and she was yanked unceremoniously to her feet…

Chapter Twenty-One
Dungeon

The constant *drip-drip-drip* of evil-smelling green water from the mouldy ceiling above her head was the only thing that provided Beth with any distraction from a headache so excruciating that it made her feel nauseous. Even just opening her eyes was almost too painful, but the suffering was not just confined to her head. Her whole body was shaking uncontrollably, partly from the icy draughts and damp stone floor she was sitting on, and also the cold iron shackles that bit tightly into her wrists and ankles. She was one throbbing mass of aches and nagging soreness, both from the explosion and everything that had happened to her over the last twenty-four hours.

There was a clanking of chains beside her, and Beth forced her eyes open. She saw Ralph examining the metalwork that bound him to the wall of the dungeon of the Tower of London, where they had been brought after being captured by the King's guards.

"Just the smallest of metal files and a bit of time – that's all it would take for me to get out of here," he said.

"Well, time's one thing we're going to have plenty of," said John wryly. He was similarly chained to the wall, and Beth saw the drying blood of an ugly cut on his forehead, marring his handsome face. "Since they think *we* were trying to kill the King, they'll never let us see the light of day again."

"Yes they will," said Ralph, sounding strangely confident. "And soon."

Beth felt something tickling her leg, and shook it violently to rid herself of the rat that had been gnawing at the hem of her dress. It scuttled away into the darkness, but not very far. She suspected the rats in this place were quite used to sharing their space with human captives.

"What makes you so sure?" she asked Ralph, frowning.

"Don't you know what this place is?"

"Well, we haven't been invited into the King's banqueting rooms," John snapped, his sense of humour long having deserted him. "It's a dungeon!"

"Not quite…" Ralph insisted.

"Oh, stop it," John groaned. "I'm tired of your stupid ways—"

"It's not just *any* dungeon, though! It's the Condemned cell," Ralph retorted ominously.

The word "condemned" struck Beth's heart like a dagger. "But we were trying to *help*! We saved the King," she said angrily. "How can they not see that?"

"Well, that's not what it looked like to them," Ralph said with a resigned sigh. "I heard one of the guards say a man with a missing finger reported that some Republican spies were going to kill the King, but panicked at the last moment when he caught them in the act."

Beth scoffed incredulously. "*Groby.* Of course," she growled through a clenched jaw.

"This is the place you're put before they take you out to the guillotine, friends. We're goners."

"How come you know so much about this place?" John demanded.

"I … I've been in here before."

"Then how did you get out? If *you* got out, *we* can!"

193

Ralph shook his head. "That was different. Someone caught me picking the lock of his strongbox in the middle of the night. After turning me in, he decided he could make use of me, and that's the only reason I got sprung out of here."

It suddenly came to Beth. "Alan Strange?"

"Who else?"

She closed her eyes again and let her head fall back against the dank wall, trying to fight back the tears of frustration welling up inside. Alan Strange had made it very clear to her that this day might come. In the dark world he inhabited there were only winners and losers, nothing in-between. This was the price losers often paid. Perhaps Strange himself had already paid it, since he had not turned up at the ringing of St Paul's bells. Had someone cracked *their* code, and worked out what the tolling of the bells meant?

Worse yet, had Strange simply used them, then abandoned them to their fate?

In her despair, Beth's mind drifted towards the theatre, whose boards she would never tread again. Who would take her parts? Someone would be found. They would mourn her passing for a time, but then life would go on and she would soon be forgotten. Worse still, perhaps they would think she really *had* been a treacherous Republican spy in their midst all along.

And then there was Maisie. How would poor, sweet Maisie manage without her? How would her young friend ever find her father without anyone to help her? Would Maisie feel compelled to see her one last time, joining the crowd that looked on as the blade came down on Beth's neck? She felt sick at the very thought.

The sound of footsteps in the corridor outside jerked Beth back into the present, and her heart quickened. Was this it? Were they already coming to take them away? She started suddenly as the door opened, and to her surprise John reached out to squeeze her hand. She smiled at him gratefully, though she could see in his eyes that he needed the comfort as much as she did.

The dungeon was so gloomy that she couldn't see who was striding across the dungeon towards them – but something about the tall, well-built outline looked familiar…

"You three are very lucky," came a deep, calm voice that Beth recognized immediately.

Alan Strange.

"Oh, indeed," said Ralph sardonically. "You've just interrupted our celebration party as it happens, Mister

 195

Strange."

The spymaster laughed softly, and it occurred to Beth that it was the first time she had ever heard him do so.

"Mister Strange? Y-you must tell the King!" John pleaded desperately. "Tell him what we were really doing! Though it would be just our luck if he wouldn't believe you either, now Edmund Groby has put about a story that—"

"The King pays me to discover the truth by any means necessary," Strange interjected calmly, holding up a hand. "And His Majesty always believes what I tell him. I have already had a private audience with him and he knows what has truly occurred. I must admit, though, that there were a few gaps in my story as I haven't had a chance to hear from you in some time—"

"Then where were you when Ralph went to St Paul's and tolled the bells?" Beth asked, her brow knitting.

"Yes, I owe you an apology. I had no idea that your signal would be summoning me for something so significant. I realize now, of course, that you must have been hoping to tell me of this plot at the Tower. I had heard the bells toll and was on my way, but then my passage was halted by an informant who told me there was a young man called Will with an urgent story to tell.

I felt I must hear his story as soon as I could – though, it transpires, even he didn't know everything…"

Beth quickly told Strange about the coded letter, Edmund Groby and their escape from the *Doodgaan*. "Will must have told you about the gunpowder on the ship, and we deduced that the coded message in that letter referred to a plot to use it here at the Tower against the King. But it was only at the last minute that we realized *where* the gunpowder was really hidden."

"And you think the letter was written by Sir Henry Vale *after* the date of his execution?" Strange said dubiously.

"I'm certain of it. It was his seal and John recognized his handwriting."

"That's true, sir. I have seen it before in my job at the Navy Board. What's more, the commissioner of the Board, Sir Roger Fortescue, is somehow involved in this along with Edmund Groby. They were both present when Arthur Jones was murdered, I witnessed them there myself. At least Fortescue shouldn't be hard to find – Beth locked him down in the cellars here just before we foiled the plot, and with any luck he hasn't been found as yet…"

Alan Strange nodded thoughtfully, not speaking for

a moment as he took all this information in. He had drawn closer to them now, and Beth could make out his rugged, battle-scarred features and the deep-set grey eyes that gave nothing away.

"You have all done well – better than I could have hoped for," he said at last. "If Vale is still alive, that is grave news indeed. He is surely the King's most cunning and dangerous enemy. A man who has the means to breach the tight security of a state execution for treason and fake his own beheading is an opponent to be respected and feared. I'm afraid we have not heard the last of him. I'm certain of requiring your help again before too long."

"Me and Beth will be ready at a moment's notice, Mister Strange – won't we, Beth?" said Ralph.

Before she could reply, Strange said, "I'm sure you will be. But as I see it, the *three* of you, all bringing different skills to bear, have succeeded in this mission. Someone with knowledge of the Navy Board, its ways and personnel, may well come in handy. Are you with us, John Turner?"

It took only the briefest glances in Beth's direction to bring John to a decision. "Yes, sir. I'm with you."

Beth exchanged a broad grin with John. A small part of her had been dreading the idea that she might not

have a reason to see him again. But now that wouldn't be a problem she was very pleased – and she could see he was too.

"So what now?" she asked the spymaster.

"Now … you shall go outside and enjoy the celebrations!" The words came not from Alan Strange, but from another figure now standing in the doorway. His voice was a clear and confident, with the hint of a French accent. As the man approached, Strange turned towards him and bowed deeply.

"Your Majesty."

Beth's heart leaped. King Charles II!

He wore a long, glistening black wig of the sort he had made fashionable since returning from exile in France, along with voluminous robes of scarlet, white and blue, and a long golden chain draped round his neck. His stockings were of pristine white silk, with royal blue garters just below the knee; a neatly trimmed black moustache decorated his upper lip.

"Mister Strange here has told me much of what has been happening of late," said His Majesty. "But I suspect that the mysterious Alan Strange doesn't even tell the *King* all – just what he needs to know. And perhaps that is for the best, otherwise I should probably be a-feared

to ever set foot out of doors!" He chuckled. "I do know, though, what you young people have done for your King and your country today, and I shall always remember it. Now, my friends, you are of course free to go. Please accept my apologies, and try to forget you were ever in this awful place. Make the most of the festivities, and if there is anything else I can do for you, you have only to ask."

"Er, there is just one small matter, Your Majesty," Ralph piped up. He held up his hands and rattled his chains loudly.

The King's hearty laughter echoed off the dungeon's stone walls as he swept out, waving one of the guards in to come and release them.

Chapter Twenty-Two

Celebrations

It was dark when Beth and the others finally stepped outside. She took in big, grateful breaths of the cold evening air and looked all about at the glow of countless bonfires dotted all over the city. The merrymaking was in full swing, with people laughing, singing and dancing around the biggest fire of them all – the one she had feared so much was going to be the source of the King's assassination earlier in the day.

"Get used to this, friends," Ralph remarked as he ambled along beside Beth and John.

"What do you mean?" John asked.

"Royal entertainments! Didn't you hear the man? We can have anything we want!"

"I don't think we were supposed to take that too literally," John cautioned. "I mean, you could try asking for your own royal palace on the banks of the Thames, but I wouldn't be building my hopes up too much if I were you!"

"I think," agreed Beth, "that we would be better off saving our favours 'til we are really in need of them."

"Aw, rats!" groaned the crestfallen Ralph.

They found themselves drawn towards the big bonfire and, in its light, Beth caught sight of the theatre manager Huntingdon and his party dancing a merry jig to a solo fiddler, with an appreciative audience looking on and clapping in time to the music. *Typical theatre folk*, she thought warmly. *Never happy unless they're the centre of attention!* Only a short while before, she had thought she might never see them again. And then Beth saw another welcome sight: Maisie was approaching, and eagerly guiding a familiar figure towards them.

"Here she is!" Maisie cried, and she and Beth exchanged hugs and fond greetings. "Will here was asking where Beth Johnson was, and I said I'd help him find you."

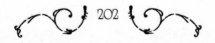

They all greeted Will fondly, glad to see he was all right. Beth introduced Maisie to John and Ralph – but then noticed that her young friend was scowling at her.

"I was *starving*, but the last I saw of you and John, you were running off with that hog roast. You disappeared out of my sight before I could even get a little mouthful of it! And then some strange bang happened and everyone started running around getting distracted—"

"Ah, sorry about that, Maisie…" Beth interjected quickly, trying not to laugh. "The hog was … um…"

"It had gone off," Ralph intervened. "Or at least it soon would have done. Would've given you terrible indigestion. They were told by the kitchen staff to get rid of it."

"Well, I was so hungry I don't think I should have minded a bit of tummy ache…" Maisie muttered.

Beth was simply relieved that her friend didn't seem to know exactly what had happened with the explosion. She put an arm round the younger girl. "Believe me, Maisie, t'would have been the death of you. Why don't you go over to Mister Huntingdon's group and tell them we'll join them anon?"

Maisie nodded, and skipped away towards the throng encircling the fire. Once she had gone, Beth turned to Will.

"We were so worried about you, Will. We *hated* leaving you on that ship…"

"It was the right thing to do. And it's worked out for the best, after all."

"It was a lucky escape, you managing to stop that fuse before the gunpowder went up!" Ralph said.

"Well, it wasn't easy thinking of a way to put out all the flames to get to it, I must say—"

Will was interrupted as they noticed that, standing on a special platform bathed in the light from the bonfire, Charles II had begun addressing the crowds.

"… and I wish to inform my subjects that today is a doubly special occasion. Not only do we celebrate the overthrow of a plot by Guy Fawkes to destroy the King and his parliament. My people, I can now reveal that this very day, a second attempt on the royal head has been made!" Gasps went up from the crowd, and the King held up his hands. "But I am pleased to say that as you can see, I still stand before you. The foul plot has been thwarted by the wit and courage of some very courageous subjects who have pledged their skills in my defence! For their sakes, their identities must remain secret, but I wish to publicly offer them my most hearty thanks…"

A great cheer went up, and continued long after the King had finished his speech and left the platform. Despite the celebrations, Beth couldn't stop herself from peering out into the darkness, wondering if Edmund Groby was out there somewhere, plotting his next move…

As the crowd returned to its revelry, Maisie ran up to join Beth and the young men, throwing her arms round her friend. Ralph, meanwhile, had returned to the question of how Will had made his escape from the ship.

"So, you have to tell us – how *did* you manage to put the fire out? The flames were so intense, and that gunpowder fuse was burning down so quickly…"

Will let out a sigh of resignation and turned to his old friend. "If you remember, John, I *had* been drinking a lot of lemonade that morning before we rowed out to the abandoned ship. And by the time you found me I *had* been chained up for a long time…"

Ralph scratched his head. "I still don't … Oh, YUCK!" he exclaimed as Beth and her friends laughed heartily.

Epilogue

Red and orange shapes flickered in the black, rippling waters of the Thames. Smoke from bonfires drifted across the river, together with the mouth-watering smell of roasting and baking, and the happy babble of hundreds of voices. There was a rustling of wings from above, and a raven took flight from the battlements of the Tower. It swooped down low over a nearby rowing boat with a harsh caw before disappearing into the darkness. A light breeze parted the smoke momentarily, revealing a man with a missing finger pulling hard on the oars of the boat, scowling up at the festivities within the grounds of the Tower of London, and another enshrouded within a great cloak and hood, sitting in the stern sheets, glaring

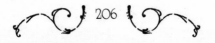

back at his oarsman.

"You failed me, Groby," said Sir Henry Vale darkly. "Now the King will know I am alive, and will stop at nothing to catch me and finish the job his executioner failed to do the last time."

"No one could have accounted for those meddling youngsters getting in the way," rasped Groby.

Vale scoffed, and turned away from his henchman in disgust. "Our mission is incomplete, and I swear to God we shall finish it." His dark eyes sparkled fiercely in the firelight as he glared towards the Tower. "If they did but know me, they would not be celebrating, but trembling in their shoes. They shall surely pay!"

~ Cast of Characters ~

BETH JOHNSON
Actress extraordinaire at the King's Theatre and –
unbeknownst to her admiring audience – a
much-valued spy. Tall and beautiful with chestnut
brown hair and green eyes, Beth has risen from lowly
depths as a foundling abandoned on the steps of Bow
Church to become a celebrated thespian and talented
espionage agent.

SIR ALAN STRANGE
Tall, dark and mysterious, spymaster Alan Strange
seeks out candidates from all walks of life, spotting the
potential for high-quality agents in the most unlikely
of places. Ruthless but fair, Strange is an inspiration for
his recruits, and trains them well.

RALPH CHANDLER
Former street urchin Ralph has lead a rough-and-
tumble existence, but his nefarious beginnings have
their uses when employed in his role as one of Sir Alan
Strange's spies, working in the service of the King.

JOHN TURNER

Junior clerk at the Navy Board, handsome John imagines himself in more daring, adventurous circumstances — and he soon has the opportunity when he meets Beth Johnson and becomes part of her gang of spies.

SIR HENRY VALE

Criminal mastermind and anti-King conspirator, Sir Henry Vale was supposedly executed by beheading in 1662 for his attempt to take the King's life — but all may not be as it seems…

EDMUND GROBY

Squat, swarthy and with one ominous finger missing from his left hand, Groby is a relentless villain and loyal henchman. He hates the monarchy and all it represents, and will stop at nothing to prevent our gang from derailing the King-killer's plans.

MAISIE WHITE

A young orange-seller at the theatre where Beth works, Maisie has been quickly taken under the older girls' wing — but she knows nothing of her friend's double life as a spy…

17th Century London

Holborn

The Strand

River Thames

Scale van een Half Engels Myl.

Moor Fields

Bishops Gate

St Pauls

Cheap Side

Aldgate

London Bridge

The Tower

Dear Reader,

I hope you have enjoyed this book. While Beth Johnson and her friends are fictitious characters, the world that they inhabit is based on history.

From 1642 to 1651, supporters of the monarchy fought against supporters of Parliament for control of England. King Charles I was executed, and Oliver Cromwell became ruler of England.

After Oliver Cromwell's rule ended, Parliament went through a troubled time. In 1660, they invited the old king's son, Charles II, to come back to England as king. However, there were still some people who hated the idea of a king running the country, and plotted to assassinate him.

Theatres had been banned in England during Oliver Cromwell's Parliament. However, when Charles II came to the throne, the ban was lifted. Drama began to thrive and women were allowed to perform on the stage. It would have been an exciting time for young actresses like Beth Johnson.

Jo Macauley

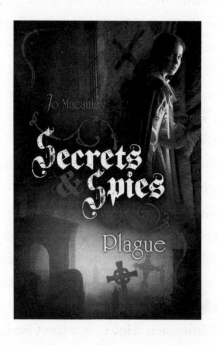

Read on for a sneak peek of the next
Secrets & Spies adventure, Plague...

Plague
London, August 1665

Death walked the streets of London, visiting households unseen in the night, and leaving bodies stiff in their sheets by morning.

The tell-tale red marks of the plague appeared without warning on living flesh, branding it as Death's own. As if the disease had been a demon or a vampire, people attempted to ward it off with herbs, prayers and mystic signs. Even learned men walked with folded abracadabra-papers in their pockets, but none of these measures seemed to slow the plague's progress.

Inside the Four Swans tavern, which lay deep in the

nested streets of the city, the atmosphere was stifling and airless. The windows were shut fast even in the baking heat of August, for fear that the stench of plague would enter and carry the disease with it. Tempers flared like hot coals, and an argument was growing loud in the half-empty bar. Already the other drinkers had begun to shift their chairs away.

Tam Dixon swigged at his ale and glared with bloodshot eyes at his two companions.

"I'll not be mocked! You're always mocking me! The pair of you, in fact. One more word and I'll crack your heads together, don't think I won't!"

"You couldn't crack the head of a louse, you great lump," sneered Martin, one of his erstwhile friends. "Sit down and drink."

Tam hesitated, swaying from the alcohol, fuming like a powder keg ready to explode. He didn't pay any attention to the thin, hollow-cheeked man who sat only an arm's length away behind him. The man had been there all evening, apparently waiting for a companion to join him – at least, that was the message implied by the hat he'd left on a neighbouring chair, as though he were saving it for someone.

Just as Tam seemed about to sit back down, a fly

settled on the lip of his beer mug.

Jack Hardy couldn't resist. "Now there's a drinker who can hold his beer better than Tam!" He roared with laughter.

The table went flying over. Mugs shattered and a serving girl gave a theatrical scream. Martin and Jack were on their feet in seconds. Tam swung for Jack first. Fist met face with a resounding smack, and as Jack went staggering back through the chairs, Martin leaped and grabbed Tam round the neck. Tam roared and swung Martin back and forth, trying to loosen the stranglehold. Martin, teeth bared, hung on grimly. In the background, Jack coughed and spat a bloodied tooth onto the floor. The thin man, meanwhile, simply sat and watched the fight happen right in front of him, as if he were too much of a fool to move out of the way. He was very good at appearing foolish.

He had put a lot of work into it while training as a spy.

Tam thumped Martin hard in the guts, finally breaking his grip. As Martin fell backward, the thin man leaped to his feet and caught him before he could hit the floor.

"Steady, there!" he said, patting Martin on the

shoulder. His other hand slipped into Martin's pocket as fast as a striking adder. The afflicted man didn't notice. Nobody did. The movement was as quick as the flicker of an eyelash, and drew about as much attention. The spy's thin fingers closed on a small piece of paper. *The prize. At last.*

Martin shoved himself away without so much as a thank you, and the spy gave an offended harrumph. Clapping his hat upon his head, he left the tavern without looking back. The paper was still in his clenched hand, curled tight as a clock spring.

One little twist of paper could do a lot of things, the spy thought to himself as he hurried through the London streets. It could entitle you to a fortune, or strip you of one. The right words, with the right signature beneath, could condemn a man to death. And once in a while, a single scrap of paper like this could be the fuse that lit the gunpowder and blew a whole city sky-high.

Moments later, the spy brushed past his master at the agreed place. The paper changed hands safely. Once his master had gone, the thin man drew out a handkerchief with shaking hands and wiped nervous sweat from his forehead. For such a tiny thing, the paper had been a monstrous weight to carry.

His heart lighter now, he made his way back through the streets, heading for home. A quick glance over his shoulder told him he wasn't being followed. If it hadn't been for the groans of the dying and the pale bodies lying unburied by the roadside, he might have whistled a merry tune.

He turned down a side street. Home was only a stone's throw away now, and he thought with relish of the cold ham and the keg of beer waiting for him…

From behind came the sound of footsteps, hurrying up swiftly.

The spy frowned. Suddenly, he was no longer sure he hadn't been followed. He was no longer sure of anything. He began to turn round, but he never saw his attacker. The last thing he felt was an agonizing blow to the head.

Then there was only the sound of a body being dragged away over the cobblestones…

Read Plague and continue
the adventure!

Look out for more
𝒮ecrets & 𝒮pies adventures…

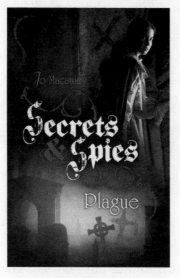

Plague

A terrible plague is sweeping through London,
and Beth and her company of actors are sent to Oxford
to entertain the King's court, which has decamped to
avoid the deadly disease. However, Beth soon finds
herself recalled to London by spymaster Alan Strange,
and together with her friends and fellow spies, she
must uncover a conspiracy that is taking advantage of
the turmoil in the capital. A conspiracy that leads right
to the seat of power…

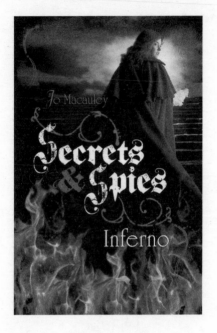

Inferno

The year is 1666 and Beth is throwing herself into a
new dramatic role a the theatre when the kidnapping of
fellow spy John's sister pulls her back into fighting the
conspiracy against the King. Henry Vale's thugs aim to
blackmail John into exposing the King, and Beth and
her friends face a race against time to rescue the young
girl – and escape the raging fire that threatens to
consume the whole city…

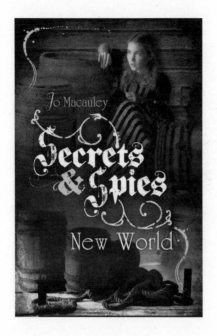

New World

When it seems Henry Vale is planning to extend his
conspiracy to kill the King to an elaborate plot in the
Americas, Beth is offered the role of a lifetime. Strange,
her spymaster, requests that Beth and her fellow spies
travel to the new world to maintain their close
surveillance of the would-be king-killer. But will their
passage across the ocean be interrupted before it
even begins?

For more exciting books from brilliant
authors, follow the fox!
www.curious-fox.com